8|21

# DATE DUE

| | | |
|---|---|---|
| BA | | |
| | | |
| | | |
| | | |
| | | |
| | | |
| | | |
| | | |
| | | |
| | | |
| | | |
| | | |
| | | |
| | | |
| | | |
| | | |
| | | |
| | | |
| | | PRINTED IN U.S.A. |

## Hayner PLD/Large Print
Overdues .10/day. Max fine cost of item. Lost or damaged item: additional $5 service charge.

# OLDER

OLDER

# OLDER

## PAMELA REDMOND

**THORNDIKE PRESS**
A part of Gale, a Cengage Company

GALE
A Cengage Company

Copyright © 2020 by Pamela Redmond.
A Younger Novel #2.
Thorndike Press, a part of Gale, a Cengage Company.

Thorndike Press® Large Print Romance.
The text of this Large Print edition is unabridged.
Other aspects of the book may vary from the original edition.
Set in 16 pt. Plantin.

LIBRARY OF CONGRESS CIP DATA ON FILE.
CATALOGUING IN PUBLICATION DATA FOR THIS BOOK
IS AVAILABLE FROM THE LIBRARY OF CONGRESS.

ISBN-13: 978-1-4328-8297-6 (hardcover alk. paper)

Published in 2021 by arrangement with Gallery Books, an imprint of Simon & Schuster, Inc.

Printed in Mexico
Print Number: 01          Print Year: 2021

To my son
Owen Redmond Satran,
who sparked this idea and fueled it the
whole way

# PROLOGUE

The night before I left the island in Maine, I made a list.

*50,* I wrote at the top of the first page in a fresh notebook.

I would celebrate my fiftieth birthday in exactly 245 days, and if I was going to do everything I needed and wanted to do before I hit that milestone, I needed to get organized. And busy. And serious.

I underscored the number *50* twice, hard.

Under *50,* I wrote *Home.*

I'd been craving a home, a real home of my own, with a new intensity. I'd enjoyed a creative and healing few years in this rustic cabin loaned to me by my publisher, Mrs. Whitney. I'd been comfortable enough before that living first with my friend Maggie, and then with my boyfriend, now ex-boyfriend, Josh.

But I was heading back to New York and I wanted a place of my own. The first place all my own I'd ever had.

*Healthy baby,* I wrote down.

My daughter Caitlin's baby, I meant. Some things were so self-evident it seemed silly to put them on the list. But scarily presumptuous not to.

*Money.*

*A job.*

*Friends.* I already had friends. But I hoped they'd be a bigger part of my life.

I'd spent the last two years getting over the previous three, and now it was time to put that phase of my life behind me. The phase in which I first pretended to be younger, and then lived as if I were, and then wrote about the whole thing. Time to grow up and own my real age, my real self, in time for the big five-oh.

I tapped my pen on the notebook. I knew what I was supposed to write next. *Relationship. Man. Dates. Love.* Or something like that.

I didn't want any of those things. Was that terrible? Did that mean there was something wrong with me? I'd spent nearly two years alone now, no man, no love, no sex. It took a while getting used to. For a long time I felt lonely, incomplete.

And then lonely turned to peaceful. Incomplete became whole, strong, perfectly

8

balanced on my own two feet.

So no, I did not aspire to be in love or engaged or married or even dating by the time I turned fifty.

Sex. Some sex would be nice. I wrote that down. Then crossed it out.

I closed the notebook and slipped it into the side pocket of my suitcase, then I got into bed with all my clothes on, including my fleece and down jacket. I turned out the lamp and lay there for a few minutes, taking in the view that had become so familiar but that I wasn't sure I'd ever see again. The cabin looked so beautiful in the light from the embers of the wood that had been burning all day in the big stone fireplace. Usually I'd throw some fresh logs on before I fell asleep, so the place would still be warm and the fire would still be alive when I woke up in the morning. But I didn't do that tonight. I wanted the coals to be cold when I left, because I wasn't coming back.

I woke up at dawn. All I had to do was tie on my boots before I set out for town and the dock and the boat to the rest of the world. April was still winter in Maine, but the temperature wasn't quite as biting as it had been, even at sunrise. I wasn't wearing gloves and I'd taken the daring step of unstrapping the cleats from my boots, given that half the ice had melted to mud.

The Volvo I'd bought when my daughter, Caitlin, was in sixth grade was waiting for me in the parking lot on the mainland. I felt like I was rewinding my life, going back to New York, back to my friend Maggie's, back to where I'd been before.

But nothing was as it had been before. Josh and I were no longer together, Maggie and Caitlin were both married, and my publishing friend Kelsey was making TV shows in LA.

TV shows, Kelsey told me via Instagram message, were the new books.

At least I had a book, the old-fashioned kind, to show for the time I'd spent on the island. Called *Younger,* it was a thinly veiled novel about the year I pretended to be a millennial. Mrs. Whitney had wanted me to write and publish it as a memoir, but as the real millennials say, I couldn't even.

That younger woman I'd been was as unreal as the character in the book. Tonight, Maggie was throwing me a party to celebrate my book and welcome me back to the city. I'd been preparing practically the entire time I'd been on the island to leave my younger life behind. I was ready. But that didn't mean, I suddenly realized, that I was ready to be older.

# ONE

I could not bring myself to blow a week's grocery money on parking, so I stubbornly drove around lower Manhattan until I found a spot on the street. The weather had changed from winter to summer in the seven hours it had taken me to drive from Maine to New York. I was wearing hiking boots and corduroys; I'd left my parka in the car and tied my fleece around my waist. By the time I dragged my suitcase the seventeen blocks to Maggie's loft, I was so drenched in sweat I looked like a contestant in a wet turtleneck contest.

"Were you in an accident?" Maggie blurted.

"I need a shower," I said.

"Oh, honey," Maggie said. "You need a lot more than a shower."

That's when I focused on the people standing behind Maggie. Apparently it was going to take a team of five — six if you

11

counted me — to pull me into shape for tonight's party.

I'd been spending a lot of time outdoors, chopping my own wood, walking three miles each way to the only store on the island. The cabin did not contain a full-length mirror or a scale, but I felt stronger and leaner than I had in years. I had all my own teeth and wore clothes I'd bought new in the past decade, which made me practically the Cate Blanchett of my little island.

"She doesn't look so bad," scolded Piper the stylist, as if I were not there.

I was about to respond with appreciation, when Piper continued, "She's got a kind of Olive Kitteridge thing going on."

Olive fucking *Kitteridge*?

"Okay, maybe I should do something with my hair," I said, touching it. I'd kind of forgotten I had hair.

"A deep-conditioning treatment and some color will make a major difference," said the hairdresser.

"I don't want to color my hair until I really need to," I told him.

"You really need to!" the group chorused.

"We'll do an intensive facial and give you some foundation to correct that redness," said the makeup artist.

The nail person clucked as she examined

my hands. Then she asked me to remove my boots and socks and got down on her knees. Until I saw her reaction, I don't think I'd ever been tempted to use the word *recoil*. She looked up at me, eyes shining with what might have been tears.

"Your poor little feet look like *hooves*," she said.

Maggie shut the double doors that walled off her and Frankie's bedroom from the rest of the loft, where a team of two florists was placing six-foot-tall magnolia branches in vintage French metal vases while the caterers set up the bar and the kids chased one another in circles as the nannies flirted with the art assistants.

In this apartment alone, I'd encountered more people in the last ten minutes than I'd seen since New Year's.

"Let's get to work," Maggie said. "We've only got five hours."

I would love to complain about those five hours, to claim that through my ascetic period living in near-isolation I'd transcended any need for physical indulgence and rejected all outer measures of worth and beauty. But I found myself dozing and possibly purring as I was lathered and scrubbed and rinsed and oiled. I was plucked and waxed and exfoliated and de-hooved.

When the team was done, I felt amazing. And looked . . . maybe not younger than when I'd walked in, but definitely better.

"Now let's find you something to wear," Maggie said.

"I'm wearing my good black dress," I said.

"You mean the one you wore to your last book party?" asked Maggie.

"She can't be seen in repeats," Piper said.

"Nobody's going to remember," I told her.

Except Josh, I reminded myself. Josh would remember. He'd been with me when I bought that black dress, the most I'd ever spent on anything without a motor. He'd assured me I looked so amazing it was worth it.

"I mean on Instagram," Piper said.

"I'm not on Instagram," I said.

"Other people will post," Piper said.

Ignoring her, I unearthed the black dress that had been lying folded in my suitcase the whole time I'd been in Maine. It seemed to have faded along the crease lines, but I decided to overlook that. All I saw was the dress in which I'd felt as happy and as beautiful as I'd ever been.

"I'm wearing this," I said.

Not because I wanted to look good for

14

Josh. We were over. So over. I'd invited him tonight to prove how completely over we were.

I stepped into the dress and zipped it up as far as I could by myself. That dress had always had the magic ability to expand and contract as I gained and lost weight, developed muscles from yoga or a paunch from too much ice cream. But now it hung on me like a black plastic garbage sack, size extra-jumbo.

"You did get skinny," said Maggie.

"They say as you get older you have to choose between your face and your ass," said Piper.

So now I was "older"? So now I'd made a choice, and my face had lost?

"You could totally rock this," Maggie said, pulling a gold minidress from Piper's over-stuffed rack.

"That's perfect," Piper said. "Very Mrs. Robinson."

I guessed Mrs. Robinson was better than Olive Kitteridge, but by then I'd transferred all my fear and loathing onto Piper and, like a rebellious thirteen-year-old, refused to even look at any of the clothes on her rack. No, not like a rebellious thirteen-year-old, like a forty-nine-year-old who could dress herself. And if anyone else didn't like it, they could bite me.

Ignoring the gold dress, I riffled through Maggie's closet until I found a pair of stretch, black leather pants and an oversized cream satin blouse.

"The shirt is Frankie's," Maggie said.

"Will they mind if I wear it?"

Maggie shrugged. "I'm sure they won't even notice."

I found my black lace bra at the bottom of my suitcase — another item that had gotten zero use on the island — and put it on underneath the shirt. Maggie and I wrestled back and forth, buttoning (me) and unbuttoning (her) the top button, until Maggie growled, "Leave the fucking button open or I'm going to rip it off."

I allowed Piper to hook on enormous gold earrings that dangled beneath my now voluminous hair. She insisted I wear her black suede heels, at least until the party got underway and nobody could see my feet anymore. There was a quick knock at the door.

"Fourteen and a half minutes till seven!" Frankie called.

A high school chemistry teacher, Frankie could be relied upon for precision.

"Right out, sweetie!" Maggie said.

But first she steered me over to the mirror, the same mirror where, five years earlier, she'd introduced me to my reconstructed twenty-six-year-old self.

My hair was thick and very brown. My face seemed to glow, but that was definitely the makeup. My outfit made me look like a restaurant hostess with a side gig as a dominatrix.

I didn't look twenty-six anymore. But I looked as close as I would ever get again.

Frankie had concocted a special *Younger* cocktail for the festivities: It involved vodka (the youngest liquor), pink champagne (girly and celebratory), and a sprig of thyme. "Time, get it?" Frankie winked.

Frankie was tall and round, with cropped strawberry blond hair and ruddy cheeks and round pale eyes magnified by thick-lensed, wide-framed glasses. Frankie was pretty much the opposite of the curvy, sultry Anna Magnani–type Maggie had always been attracted to. They were also the temperamental opposite of Maggie's usual fiery, high-drama partners: calm, patient, soft-spoken, supportive. Maggie had never been happier.

Maggie had invited everyone she knew to the party, and many people she didn't, thanks to the prodigious connections she now enjoyed as a famous artist. (She tried to make me put quotes around that term, but she had genuinely become a famous artist.)

The elevator doors opened, spilling a new carload of people into the apartment, including one person who stood a head above everyone else. That was my son-in-law, Ravi, a medical resident who had once played semipro basketball in Germany. My eyes traveled down to his shoulder where stood my daughter, Caitlin, as petite as her husband was tall, as fair as he was dark. She and Ravi had announced their pregnancy when I was visiting in December, for Maggie's and my joint birthday and the winter holidays. Caitlin had been barely pregnant then and had looked more drawn than full, but I caught my breath now when she whispered something in Ravi's ear and I saw her distinctly rounded belly. My little baby, expecting a baby.

I pushed through the crowd, intent only on getting to her.

"Wow, Mom, you're wearing as much makeup as a Kardashian," Caitlin said.

If there had been a sink right there, I would have washed my face, but I had to settle for sucking it up and giving my daughter a hug.

"Maggie thought I needed a makeover.

You look amazing, honey."

She ran a caressing hand over her belly.

"I felt her move today," she said, excitement dancing in her eyes.

"Her?" I said. This was news.

"They don't know for sure," said Ravi.

"Officially we don't want to know," corrected Caitlin. "And seriously, all I can worry about is whether the baby has two heads or if its little heart will keep beating."

"You're past the danger point," Ravi said.

"I don't know if you're ever past the danger point," I said.

"You were what, six months pregnant when you had your second miscarriage?" said Caitlin.

"Seven," I said.

Caitlin was five when that happened, old enough to know that Mommy had a baby in her tummy but now the baby was gone. Old enough to try to comfort me when I was crying.

Ravi shot me a dark look. "The doctor said everything looked fine," Ravi said.

"I'm sure he's right," I hurried to reassure my daughter.

"She," said Caitlin. "Jeez, Mom, don't be such a sexist!"

"I'll make you a plate of fruit and vegetables," I said. "Let's find a place for you to sit."

Ravi took Caitlin's arm. "We're going to say hello to Maggie," he said, firmly steering my daughter away.

I stood there feeling abandoned for only a second before I felt two arms slip around me from behind. I swung around to see the beaming face of my old friend and colleague Kelsey Peters. Kelsey and I had worked together at Empirical Press before she'd moved first to France and then to Hollywood to become a television producer.

"I can't believe you made it!" I said, pulling her into a hug.

Kelsey was such a strong person, I always forgot how tiny she was; her head barely reached my chin. Now in her midthirties, she looked older, but in the best possible way. When we worked together in New York, she'd favored a tightly laced, ambitious-career-woman look: pencil skirts, pointy high heels, bright red lips, and twice-weekly blowouts. Living in her native California had made her look at once softer and more sophisticated, with her tousled blond hair, flowing embroidered blouse, vintage jeans, lace-up boots, and Gucci bag.

"I had to be here," she said. "I love the book."

"Really?" I said, genuinely pleased.

Kelsey was still the best editor I'd ever worked with. She'd edited my first two novels, one a coming-of-age love story and the other a highly fictionalized account of three moms in crisis. The whole time I'd been writing *Younger,* I could hear her voice in my head urging me to find a fresher metaphor, a more vivid description, a truer feeling.

"Absolutely," Kelsey said. "I told Mrs. Whitney I wished I'd been the editor."

Kelsey and I both looked over to where our former boss, Mrs. Whitney, was holding court on the long, low sofa. Beside her sat the white Hermès bag that held her little white dog, Toto, which matched her thick white hair, brushed straight back from her forehead. She was wearing a black-and-white Chanel jacket she'd had since I first worked at Empirical Press in the '90s.

"As long as you felt okay about your character," I said.

"Are you kidding? I've been going around telling everybody Lindsay is me. What did Josh think?"

"Josh and I haven't been in touch," I said stiffly.

"I'm sorry to hear that. I always thought he was a great guy."

21

Kelsey had known Josh for almost as long as I had, and had encouraged me from the beginning to get more serious with him, to get married and have babies, not knowing I was fifteen years older than Josh and had already spent a lifetime as a suburban wife and mother.

"I invited him tonight. I thought it was time for us to be friends again."

"That's very grown-up of you," Kelsey said.

"Thank you, but apparently he didn't agree, because he's not here."

"Well, if he shows up, say hi for me. I'm sorry to do this but I've got to run. I got last-minute house seats for Sutton Foster's one-woman show."

"Oh, that's amazing. Caitlin took me to see it in December as a combo holiday-birthday present."

"Do you have time to get together tomorrow to talk about the book? Bemelmans at five?"

Bemelmans Bar at The Carlyle, with the murals painted by the artist who'd created the Madeline books, had always been Kelsey's and my special place, reserved for celebrating major book deals or mourning long-term breakups or announcing life-changing news. Or, I guess, publishing new books and seeing each other for the first time in more than three years.

"Perfect."

There was the sound of a spoon clinking on glass, Kelsey's cue to duck out of sight. A hush fell over the crowd. Maggie motioned me to her side and began saying nice things about me and my book. I scanned the crowd. Still no sign of Josh. Just as well, I supposed. Maybe he was smarter than me, maintaining the distance that had grown between us.

Judging from the silence and the fact that everyone was staring at me, it was my turn to talk. So I stood there and explained how writing the book had helped me understand a challenging and amazing passage of my life. I thanked people and joked that the afternoon's beautifying routine had made me look forty-six instead of forty-nine.

And then Josh walked in and all the words flew out of my head. He looked different, his cheeks more angular, his shoulders wider, a new crease between his eyes. And something else I couldn't pinpoint that transformed him from an overgrown boy to a fully grown man. My stomach dropped into my vagina.

Oh no. Oh no no no no. Getting over him

was why I'd spent two years alone on an island in Maine turning into a pillar of salt. Getting over him was why I'd written this highly personal and potentially hugely embarrassing book. Getting over him was why I'd oh so coolly sent him a Paperless Post invitation to this party.

But this did not feel like I was over him.

"So, yeah, I wrote this book," I said, trying not to look at him, but unable to look anywhere else. "I think maybe you can buy it here."

Could you? If so, where? It was a big loft. "Or maybe not."

People were still looking at me, somewhat uncertainly.

"Goodbye," I said. I knew that wasn't right. But it did the job: To my enormous relief, everyone went back to talking to one another.

I managed to forget about Josh for a few minutes as people nicely asked me to sign books. But when the last person handed me a book to sign and I looked up to ask their name, it was Josh.

"Hey, thanks for coming," I said.

Sounding like a somewhat normal human being. A sane, calm person with only a slight quaver in her voice.

"Of course," he said. "I was really happy

24

you invited me."

Then we stood there smiling at each other for way too long.

"The book's awesome," he said finally.

"Oh, good." I was sincerely relieved. The lawyers had sent him advance proofs, so I knew he'd read it and officially signed off, but he hadn't said anything to me. "Is that what you really thought?"

"Are you in the city for a while? I'd love to talk to you about it."

"I just moved back," I said.

"Wow," he said. "Amazing. Are you staying here with Maggie?"

"Until I find a place," I said.

Which hopefully would be soon. Maggie had expanded to take over two entire floors of the building, but she filled every inch with her art studio and her enormous egg sculptures and her growing family and her army of assistants and domestic helpers. She'd given me my own tiny room, but that meant the day nanny and the night nanny had to share.

"My new office is nearby," he said. "I'd love to show it to you."

"I'd love to see it," I said.

The word *love* was getting thrown around a bit more than made me comfortable. I lifted my hair off my neck, licking my lips and sneaking a look at Josh from under my eyelashes. Feeling awfully glad Maggie had made me leave that top button open.

What the fuck was I doing? I dropped my hair and shook my head. I knew for sure that I did not want Josh back. But I somehow felt compelled to act as if I did.

"Babe." A beautiful woman, tall, thin, with skin the same tawny shade of brown as her hair and her eyes, glided up — she seemed not to need normal legs — and slung her arm around Josh's shoulders.

"Oh, hey!" He seemed happy to see her. "This is the famous Liza," he told her. And then to me, he said, "Liza, this is Zen."

She stuck out her long, thin, bronze hand. "Josh's fiancée," she clarified.

I noticed her ring then. It was a simple platinum band set with an oval emerald, roughly the size of a grape. She pressed herself close to Josh and kissed him on the neck. Was that really necessary?

"I need to go, babe," she said. "Were you coming or . . . ?"

"Great to see you, Josh," I said quickly.

Please leave. Please don't make me stand here feeling both turned on and rejected by you for one more excruciating second.

"I'll text you about visiting the office," he said.

"Alrighty," I said.

Alrighty? What was I, a 1950s bobby-soxer?

I tried again. "Alrighty, then."

That was worse. I could feel my cheeks blazing.

And then burning even hotter as Josh leaned over and kissed me goodbye. With the touch of his lips, he undid two years of denial and sublimation. Now you have to make me unwant you, Josh. Make me unwant you all over again.

27

# TWO

The waiter set down two icy gin martinis, straight up, three olives. As if we were members of a synchronized drinking team, Kelsey and I lifted them in a toast.

"Here's to getting what you want," Kelsey said.

"Here's to knowing what you want," I said.

"I know what I want," Kelsey said, taking a generous sip. "I want a baby. I just can't find somebody to impregnate me."

"Oh, come on. Who wouldn't want to have babies with you?"

"All the guys in LA who are my age plan to work sixteen hours a day until they're in their late forties, when they'll be rich and powerful enough to marry a superhot twenty-two-year-old who'll have lots of babies and no career of her own," Kelsey said.

"So who does that leave for you?"

"Guys in their late fifties who've already had their families," she said, "or younger men who think you can help them with their careers."

We both took long swallows of our drinks.

"Well, who needs a man?" I said. "If you really want to have a baby, have a baby. Look at Maggie and Frankie."

Maggie had gotten pregnant with her daughter Celia via donor sperm, and then midway through the pregnancy had adopted one-year-old Edie from China. Before Maggie and Frankie met, Frankie had gone off their hormones in order to get pregnant and bear a child — Oliver, who was always called Ollie. Ollie was now seven, Edie six, and Celia five.

"All props to them, but I just don't think I can handle that," Kelsey said. "I work all the time, I'm away on shoots for weeks or months, and I can't imagine having anything like a normal family life without a partner."

"I get it," I said. "Josh showed up at the party last night with his gorgeous supermodel fiancée, who I'm sure he's fixing to have babies with."

"That sucks," she said. "What did you do?"

"Felt terrible all night. I mean, I was the one who left him. I left because he wanted kids and I didn't, so I should be cool with it, right?"

"Are you having second thoughts?"

"Not about having babies, no, that door is nailed shut for me. But I couldn't help feeling jealous, and I kept *flirting* with him . . ."

"You two always had a lot of chemistry," Kelsey said.

"I was acting like a teenager. And I'm about to be a *grandmother.*"

"Yeah, yeah, but you're not *dead,*" Kelsey said.

"He's a cute boy," I admitted, "and maybe he's the love of my life. But I can't let myself slide right back into that. It's time I make a life of my own, get my own place, a new job . . ."

"A job?" Kelsey looked amused but baffled, as if I had expressed a desire to get a pet lamb, or a tattoo of a hula dancer. "What kind of job?"

"I'm going to see Mrs. Whitney later this week. I'd like to go back and work at Empirical."

She frowned. "What about writing? That was always your dream."

"I love writing, but it's really lonely. I want to work with people again," I told her. "Plus I can't make enough money writing novels to live in New York."

30

"Why do you want to live in New York?" Kelsey said. "It's expensive, it's crowded, it's fucking freezing." She gave a little shiver for effect. "Come to LA. The weather's great and everybody's got these charming guest houses where you can live for cheap."

"I've got to be near Caitlin now. She's really anxious about this pregnancy, and I promised her I'd do what I can to help."

Kelsey leaned forward, eyes shining. "I've got something I need to talk with you about," she said.

I knew that look. It was the look Kelsey used to get when she'd read a short story in an obscure literary journal she was sure could be a brilliant novel, or when she came up with a scheme to win the hottest book auction of the season. The best you could do when Kelsey got that look was hold tight and hope she took you along for the ride.

"I want to turn *Younger* into a TV show," she said.

Wow. That was unexpected. Kelsey's background in publishing meant that most of the TV projects she'd done had been vintage literary specials, adaptations of Jane Austen and Miss Marple.

"That's really nice of you," I said carefully, afraid she was trying to help me out but wasn't really interested in the project,

31

"but isn't *Younger* a little . . . frothy for you?"

"That's exactly what I love about it," she said. "It's light, it's fun, it's commercial, and it's also got a deeper message. Yeah, I've been doing these serious period dramas, but I need a big fucking *hit.*"

"That sounds . . . amazing," I said. "But I'm not sure I know what this all means."

"It doesn't mean anything right now," she told me. "I have to make a deal with your agent for the option, which is not going to be a lot of money, I have to warn you: a few thousand dollars. Then I package it and shop it around to find the financing and the clout to get it made."

"Who will you take it to?" I asked. I had no idea how this worked.

"Networks. Studios. Stars. I didn't want to tell you this before I was sure, but that's why I went to see Sutton Foster last night. I talked to her after the show and gave her your book. She already texted me: She loves it."

"Wow" was all I managed to say. It was as if a rare butterfly had landed on the table between us and I had to be really careful not to crush it. "What do I need to do now?"

"Nothing," she said. "Just sell me the rights to your brilliant book. I promise I'll turn it into a show you'll be proud of."

I was about to say that of course I'd sell her the rights to my book, that there was no one I'd trust more with it, when I remembered something. Something that could be a problem.

"I have to talk to Mrs. Whitney first," I said.

Kelsey frowned. "What does Mrs. Whitney have to do with it?"

"We share the film and television rights. I have one of those contracts."

"Shit," Kelsey said. "I forgot about that."

Mrs. Whitney was famously particular about the books she published being adapted into movies or television shows. She'd had a bad experience years ago, so insisted on sharing the rights with the author. And she usually said no.

"Should I talk to her?" Kelsey said.

"I'll bring it up when I see her this week."

"Okay. I'm going back to LA tomorrow," she said, "but I won't do anything until I hear from you."

I picked up the metaphorical butterfly and gently placed it in my purse. I could hear its wings fluttering in there, nearly hear its heart beating, but until I talked with Mrs. Whitney, I wouldn't be able to let it take flight.

# THREE

On Sunday I went with Caitlin out to
Brooklyn to tour open houses. Caitlin and
Ravi lived in a one-bedroom apartment and
needed to find a bigger place before the
baby was born, less than four months from
now. Their current bedroom didn't even fit
a dresser, never mind a bassinet, and they
ate their meals sitting shoulder to shoulder
on a love seat. There was no way they could
fit another person into that apartment, even
one who weighed less than ten pounds.

Caitlin and I wandered with at least
twenty other people around the top floor of
a Brooklyn brownstone, reconfigured into a
two-bedroom apartment now for sale at
$1.2 million. The walls were painted white,
the kitchen cupboards shellacked a deep
blue, and all the hardware was black. The
bathroom was a mix of white subway tile,
black hardware, and a black-and-white
geometric floor.

There was an antique marble mantel in the living room, but no fireplace. The hallway held a stacked washer and dryer, but the second bedroom had a skylight instead of a window and was smaller than Caitlin's childhood closet.

Before we left, Caitlin swiped a brochure from the slate countertop, along with the real-estate agent's card. I heard other people asking when bids were due.

"That place was so expensive," I said, halfway down the stairs.

Caitlin looked surprised. "I was going to say it was cheap."

It was the fifth open house we'd been to that day. All the apartments were roughly the same amount of space, the same design.

"Are you thinking about bidding on it?" I asked carefully.

"Maybe," she said. "The light was beautiful. And did you see the skylight in the bedroom?"

"You can't let in air through a skylight," I said. "And living on the top floor would be really hard with a baby."

"It keeps you in shape."

"Where do you park the stroller? Do you leave the baby upstairs alone when you run down to sign for a package? Do you really want to walk up and down three flights with

35

a one-year-old who could go flying any minute —"

"Mom, stop!"

We were outside at the top of the stoop by then. It was a beautiful spring weekend day. Families were parading up and down the sidewalk, pushing strollers, walking dogs, shepherding children who whizzed along on scooters.

"Sorry," Caitlin said. "You're right. And that place was too small for us anyway."

We picked our way down to the sidewalk and joined the throng walking toward Fort Greene Park.

"That's why we moved to Homewood when I was pregnant with you," I said. "Have you considered New Jersey?"

Caitlin stopped stock-still in the middle of the sidewalk, forcing everyone to detour around us. "Let me make something clear, Mother," she said. Your kid calling you "Mother" is like your mother calling you by your full name when you're a kid: *Get down here right this instant, Elizabeth Margaret.* "I will *never* move to New Jersey."

"Okay," I said, chastened.

"Nothing against New Jersey," Caitlin said.

"Of course not. I love New Jersey."

"It's just that I want our child to have a

36

more diverse upbringing," said Caitlin.

"Right. The challenge is to find a big enough place you can afford in the city."

Caitlin got a mysterious little smile on her face. Pregnant, she looked ironically more like her little girl self, cheeks softer, body cuddlier. She took my arm and we started walking again toward the park.

"There is one more place I'd love to show you," she said.

We skirted the park and headed down DeKalb Avenue, past the restaurants thronged with Sunday revelers. Every place had set tables and chairs right out on the sidewalk, so that it felt like one continuous New York party.

The restaurants thinned out and then we reached the Pratt campus. We zigzagged from there down leafy streets and finally stopped outside a three-story wooden building, its pale blue paint peeling, the stone front stoop blocked off with yellow tape. In front was a FOR SALE sign; a young couple who looked like those at the other open houses emerged from the garden-level door under the stoop.

"Are you interested in this house?" I said to Caitlin, surprised. All the places we'd seen so far had been heavily renovated, but this place looked like it needed ten- or fifteen-years' worth of work.

Inside, it was in even worse shape than I'd guessed: walls torn down to the studs, pipes and electricity bared, rough floorboards covered with caked mud.

But it also had a lot of vintage charm: petite fireplaces with original marble mantels in each room and porcelain fixtures in the two bathrooms.

The garden floor held a rudimentary kitchen and what might have been — in the nineteenth century — a maid's room, off which a closet had been converted to a room with a toilet but no sink. The parlor floor was made up of a living room and dining room, both with fireplaces, and on the second floor were three bedrooms, all tiny by modern standards. Ravi might have to sleep with his feet hanging out into the hallway.

"What do you think?" Caitlin asked.

"It's a lot," I said.

"I know, it needs work."

"Money, too."

"But it could be great, don't you think?"

"It could," I agreed. At one point in my life, I would have loved to have gotten my hands on a place like this and restored it to its former glory.

"I was having this fantasy that maybe we

38

could buy it together," Caitlin said.

"Who's 'we'?" I said in all innocence.

"You and me and Ravi!" Caitlin said excitedly. "We could all go in on the down payment, and then I was thinking maybe you could advance us the money for the renovation and do all the design work. You're so good at that."

"But Caitlin," I said. "I don't have any money."

Caitlin looked as stunned as I felt. "By no money, you mean . . ."

I hadn't hidden my financial situation from my daughter, exactly, but I hadn't talked to her about it either. My advance for *Younger* had been less than it had cost me to live during the time it took to write and edit it, even considering the free rent at Mrs. Whitney's cabin. And then I'd spent most of what I had left in savings on Caitlin and Ravi's wedding last summer. I hadn't wanted that to weigh on her or compromise her happiness. But the bottom line was that I had less than fifteen thousand dollars left in my retirement account.

"I've got to get a job so I can afford to rent a crappy apartment," I said.

"But if we all lived together," said Caitlin, "you could take care of the baby and do your writing, and then I could go back to work full-time so we could afford to stay in the city."

I had always envisioned myself spending as much time as possible with my daughter's baby. But eight a.m. to six or seven p.m. five days a week? Maybe not that much time.

"Oh, Caitie," I said. "I would love to be able to do that, but I need a job with health insurance and a regular salary that pays me enough to live on. I have a meeting set up with Mrs. Whitney this week to talk about going back to Empirical."

"I knew you'd think I should stay home with the baby," my daughter said. "That I shouldn't go back to work."

"What?" How had she gotten there? "No. That's not it at all."

"Because you stayed home, you think I should stay home."

"No! I don't think that! If anything, the opposite. I didn't intend to be a stay-at-home mom."

"You didn't?" said Caitlin.

I was sure she'd heard this story, but maybe it hadn't felt so relevant before.

"When we moved to New Jersey, I thought I'd try to have another baby right away and then go back to work, but I lost that pregnancy. . . ."

"That was the late miscarriage?"

"No, the first one was before three months," I said. "And then I didn't get pregnant again, so we started going through infertility treatments. It was the second miscarriage that was late. . . ."

Caitlin looked terrified. "Is that going to happen to me?" she asked. I saw then that her eyes were shiny with potential tears.

"No, sweetheart, *no*. It's not anything I did or anything you can inherit. Sometimes it just happens. The point is, by the time I stopped trying to have another kid, I'd already been home for ten years and it felt too late to go back."

"I always thought you wanted to be home," Caitlin said.

Ouch.

"I *did* want to be home," I assured her. "I *loved* being there with you. But I missed a big chunk of my career, and you know how hard it was for me to go back."

"But I also know how nice it was having you stay home with me. Growing up, I always thought I'd want that for my child."

I put my arm around my daughter. "So do that if you want. Or go back to work if you want. There are lots of great childcare options out there. Your choice doesn't have to be dependent on me."

41

"I don't know if I can leave a newborn with a stranger," Caitlin said.

This begged one obvious question. "What about Ravi?" I said.

"Once Ravi finishes his residency, he's going to make a lot more money than me," Caitlin said. "He's also up for this big fellowship. He says he'll help out with childcare, but he doesn't really have time to do that much."

That was probably realistic. Caitlin's father, just starting his dental practice when she was born, had said the same thing. It was so self-perpetuating: Men had more ambitious and lucrative careers, which cast them as breadwinners rather than caregivers, which made them more successful and higher earners, while the parent staying home lost professional ground every year.

I wanted to be there for my daughter. I wanted to support her and encourage her to go back to work if that's what she wanted, because I knew it wasn't going to be easy, no matter what choice she made. But I also knew that having a baby was like entering a long dark tunnel that opened into an unfamiliar and unpredictable world from which you might never emerge. From which you might never want to emerge.

Becoming a parent was like being a baby

all over again, like going from the cozy familiarity of your adult life, through a difficult passage to a new incarnation where you often felt ignorant and overwhelmed. On the precipice, that passage looked much more terrifying to me than it had the first time, now that I'd experienced how life-altering it was, how all-consuming.

I had contemplated entering it again before, when Josh had told me he wanted to have children after all. And I knew I could not go in, not again. And I was even more sure of that now.

But how could I leave my daughter to enter it alone? Ravi sometimes worked twenty-four-hour shifts and was often on call, an unreliable support. Caitlin's father lived way out in Pennsylvania with a new wife and young stepchildren of his own. She needed somebody, and I was who she had.

"Let's see how it goes," I told her. "I don't know what's going to happen with Mrs. Whitney. And there's this other possibility, of Kelsey turning *Younger* into a television show."

"What?" Caitlin yelped. "I mean, that sounds amazing; I'm really happy for you. But would that mean you have to move to LA?"

"Of course not. Don't be silly. It's way

premature to worry about what any of this would mean, but I'm not going anywhere."

"I'm sorry," Caitlin said. "My hormones are making me crazy. I'm going to have this tiny person who'll be completely dependent on me and I'm terrified of screwing it up."

I gathered my daughter into my arms. Every mother knows that feeling. You never really get over it. You just learn to live with the tension between needing to create an ideal world for your child and knowing that's ultimately beyond your power.

"It's going to be okay," I told her, not because I knew it would be, or because I could make it so, but because at least I could help her feel more confident.

"Promise you'll be here for me," she said into my shoulder.

"I'll always be here for you," I said.

*Even,* I added to myself, *when I'm not here.*

# FOUR

I had always idolized and feared Ruth Whitney, the head of Empirical Press, in equal measure. She was like a queen to me, remote and awe-inspiring when I worked for her company right out of college, a role model when I again got a job with Empirical as my fake younger self.

*Someday,* I always thought, *when I grow up, I want to be just like Mrs. Whitney.*

The trouble with Mrs. Whitney was that she always seemed light-years ahead of anyplace I thought I could go or anyone I could possibly be. When I first worked for her more than twenty-five years ago, I estimated she was about seventy years old, but now she still looked seventy to me. She was old-school establishment, with her Chanel suits and her social club memberships, but she was also a rule-breaker and an iconoclast, building her publishing company to be more independent in an era

45

when all the competition was becoming more corporate.

She and I had gotten closer since she became my editor with *Younger* and loaned me her cabin in Maine. She'd bought that place with her husband in the '60s — no one I knew had ever met Mr. Whitney, who'd died long ago — and had spent summer holidays and the month of August there until a few years before, when the trip became too difficult for her.

Staying there had opened the door to a new level of closeness between us, albeit one that existed mostly in my mind. When you've slept in somebody's bed, paged through their books, eaten from their plates, as I did in Maine, you got to know them in an intimate way. Mrs. Whitney felt like a kind of mother to me, albeit one who was not very motherly.

I always dressed up for our lunches, which invariably took place at the Colony Club, the first New York social club for women, housed in a beautiful and imposing brick-and-marble building on Park Avenue. Today, though, Mrs. Whitney suggested we meet at the Empirical Press offices. Her longtime assistant, Betty, all blond frizzy hair and solicitousness, led me past an alarming number of empty desks back to Mrs. Whitney's private office.

Mrs. Whitney still had a knockout view, even if there were at least three new skyscrapers going up between her and the river. And the room was vast and sumptuous with its white linen sofas and cream carpet, though both looked undeniably dingier than I remembered from the last time I was here.

"Darling," Mrs. Whitney said, kissing me on each cheek at least two times. "Thank you for that *lovely* party the other night. I had an absolutely *fabulous* time."

"Thank you for publishing me a beautiful book," I said.

She led me over to one of the long white sofas, perching on one end while indicating that I should sit across from her. From here I had a perfect view through the glass wall that separated Mrs. Whitney's private sanctum from the half-deserted main office.

"Is this BEA week?" I asked, confused.

The big BookExpo took place in New York at the end of May every year, which would explain the unoccupied desks. But that was nearly a month away.

"Oh no. We've been paring back," Mrs. Whitney said breezily. "Slimming down, professionally speaking. Focusing more on what's really important to us."

"Oh," I said, surprised. "I'd love to hear

more about that."

"Shall we order some lunch?" Mrs. Whitney said.

She slid a menu from Burger Barn across the white marble coffee table.

"No Colony Club?" I said, trying not to sound disappointed, which I was surprised to find I was. It was so much fun to complain about those elaborate lunches, but also so much fun to have them. I had always been embarrassed to make the waiter in white gloves use his silver utensils to pick me a piece of lobster, but now I really missed it.

"So stuffy," she said, accurately. "Besides, I don't know anyone there anymore."

That was patently untrue. When you went to lunch with Mrs. Whitney at the Colony, so many people had so much to say to her that you could barely get a word in edgewise. In that sense, I was glad we were lunching at the office.

"I'm glad to get you to myself," I said.

I ordered a grilled cheese and tomato, my standing order when Kelsey and I lunched regularly at the Burger Barn, and Mrs. W. ordered a Cobb salad with dressing on the side. At the Colony, the Cobb had always been her favorite. I had a feeling the Burger Barn version may not live up to that standard, though Mrs. Whitney would undoubtedly repress and deny any disappointment.

I waited until the lunch had arrived and the Cobb dressing dispensed with entirely — "It's quite all right! Much better for the waistline!" — to make my pitch.

"I'd really like to hear what you have planned for Empirical," I said, "because I'm hoping you'll hire me back again."

Mrs. W.'s fork paused in midair.

"You want to come back and work here?" she said. "In a job?"

"Yes, that's what I was hoping. After writing three novels, I'd love to specialize in editing women's fiction, but I could handle some nonfiction too."

"No," Mrs. Whitney said.

I thought there would be more. There wasn't.

"No . . . ?" I said.

"No, there are no jobs," Mrs. Whitney said. "Not just for you, for anyone. I can do with freelancers who live in Amagansett or Seattle what it used to take a whole office full of people on salary to do."

"Well, maybe I can freelance," I said. "I can edit from home. . . ."

"But you were never really an editor, were you?" Mrs. Whitney said. "I seem to remember you worked in marketing."

49

"Marketing gave me a good sense for how to package books to maximize sales," I said, grasping. "That, plus my writing experience . . ."

Mrs. Whitney reached across the coffee table and laid a hand gently on my knee.

"I'm sorry," she said.

Frankly, I was thrown. I had no plan B. But I could certainly manufacture one.

"Then maybe we should talk about a new book," I said. "I have an idea for another novel."

"No," Mrs. Whitney said.

"You don't want to publish what I write, either?"

"It's not that I don't want to publish what you write. I love your writing. I'm just not interested in novels these days."

"What are you interested in?" I asked.

"Reality," she said. "Do you want to write a book about what it's like to be fifty in America today? That's one I might be interested in publishing."

"Maybe," I said, only because I couldn't say a flat no. But I'd never written nonfiction or read it, either. Plus I had no idea what it was like to be fifty in America.

"But I can't give you an advance," she said.

I glanced back at the empty office. I'd

50

been loath to bring this up directly, but I couldn't ignore it any longer.

"Is there some problem?" I said, feeling my heart pick up speed. "Is the company in . . . some kind of financial trouble?"

"No, no, nothing like that," she said. "I just find as time goes on that I have less patience for doing anything I don't really want to do. Life is too short, as they say."

I took a deep breath. There was still the issue of the TV show. Though I felt even more nervous asking her about this now than I had when I walked in.

"There is something else," I said. "I know in the past you haven't been keen on this sort of thing, but Kelsey wants to turn *Younger* into a TV series."

"Kelsey?" she said. "*Our* Kelsey?"

"Yes, she's a producer in LA now."

"She talked to me about that at the party," Mrs. Whitney said. "Why someone with her intelligence and talent would go into the television business is beyond me."

"I guess that's where the money is," I said awkwardly. I was already bracing myself for the third and final no.

"She mentioned she'd worked on a Jane Austen adaptation," Mrs. Whitney said. "Is that the kind of thing she has in mind for *Younger*?"

I would really have liked to have been able to say yes. But I could not lie to my idol.

"I think she's thinking of something more like a . . ." I was trying to think of another word for this but could not. ". . . situation comedy?"

Mrs. Whitney astonished me by breaking into applause.

"Would that be a popular show?" she asked eagerly. "The kind of show that could sell a lot of books?"

"I suppose so," I said.

"Then I'm all for it," said Mrs. Whitney. "Tell her the answer is yes."

I was so relieved. I told Mrs. Whitney I'd been afraid she wouldn't want to do the show. "Why on earth not?" she said.

"I thought you'd be worried it might sully your literary reputation?" I ventured. "Undermine how people would think of Empirical's books in the future?"

"The future?" Mrs. Whitney said. "We can't control the future. All we have is now."

I didn't even wait until I was out on the street to text Kelsey: *Mrs. W said yes!*

Kelsey responded immediately with enough thumbs up and hands clapping to fill my screen.

# FIVE

Josh invited me to meet at his office at five on Thursday.

*Show you around,* he texted. *Catch up.*

Being a mature, sensible person who was certainly capable of having a friendly relationship with her ex, I agreed.

It was a good thing we didn't meet until five, because it took me all afternoon to get dressed. After never once wearing leather pants in my entire life, I now seemed to find them suitable for every occasion. I blow-dried my hair and put lipstick on, then wiped it off three times. Looking effortlessly hot took a lot more effort than it used to.

The problem with Josh was that he actually did look effortlessly hot. He was wearing an old tee shirt I'd personally slept with my nose pressed against, and the loose jeans that perennially looked as if they were about to slip off his slim hips. He also had on his studious, horn-rimmed James Dean glasses, which made him look the way they made James Dean look: even more heartbreakingly handsome than usual.

I reached out my hand to shake his.

"Come here," he said, opening his arms. I walked into them like a zombie bride.

He felt so good, he looked so good, I wanted him like a chocolate chip cookie at the end of a long diet, and as with the cookie, I also knew that having him would be a huge mistake. Slippery slope.

Plus, I didn't want him! I didn't in theory and I didn't even standing there in his arms. But I was craving him, and I knew being with him would feel so good. Did I want him because I was lonely, because I was angry, because I wanted to prove I could take him away from his young girlfriend? Yes, probably all of the above.

As he showed me around the office, I tried to focus on the huge arched windows that had been restored and on the specially polished concrete floors, but all I could really think about was how I wanted two very different relationships with the same person at the same time. I wanted, like some mythical villainess, to throw him down on the floor and have my way with him, then discard him to the fires of hell. But I also wanted to reclaim the easy camaraderie of old friends happy to be back in touch.

"So what do you think?" he said.

I nearly bumped into him. He stood there with a large goofy grin on his face.

"It's . . . fantastic," I said, hoping that was a reasonable response to whatever the hell he was talking about. "I'm just not sure I understand what exactly you *do.*"

Josh had traded tattoo artistry for digital startups when we were still together, but none of his businesses had ever made any sense to me.

To my relief, he laughed. I loved his laugh.

"We put all your information in your own hands," he said. "Your data is out there, people are trading it, making money from it, but if anyone should be able to license it for profit, it's you."

I got a shiver. It was Etsy for the soul!

"You are going to be so fucking rich," I said.

I wanted to marry him.

I wanted to punch him.

"Right now we're testing a free model, like Unsplash," he said, as if I should know what that meant. "We'll give people free access to their information, if they let us use it to hyper-target advertising on our own site. Later we'll introduce a paid model where you can track what's happening with your data in real time, get alerts when new information about you is posted or accessed, and even auction your data to multiple bidders."

"How much would somebody pay for the data of a lonely middle-aged woman with a thing for younger guys?" I joked.

Could somebody please just laser me unconscious?

"Uh, that could go for a lot," he said, his cheeks tingeing pink. "Do you want to go up on the roof?"

Did a starving woman want a chocolate chip cookie?

The roof had a proper deck, with views of the harbor and the green glint of the Statue of Liberty peeking from the side of one of the new skyscrapers. There was also a mini fridge and a self-service bar and modern sofas angled to catch the setting sun.

Josh got out a bottle of champagne and approached the sofa, holding two champagne flutes. Holy shit, what was happening?

"I wanted to tell you how much I loved the book," he said.

"Oh." I felt relieved, and a little bit deflated. "So you were okay with the Josh character?"

Josh had made me promise, back when I

first started writing, that if I ever wrote about him, I'd use his real name and tell the whole truth.

"Everything about me was fine," he said. He handed me the flutes and began wrestling with the champagne cork. As it released with a soft pop, he said, "But there were some things in there I didn't know about you."

We'd gotten back together after our first breakup and lived together for two years. We'd planned to get married. I thought he'd known everything about me.

"Like what?" I said.

He filled both glasses, then set down the bottle and took one of the glasses for himself. I felt his pinky brush my hand.

"I had no idea you felt so terrible about lying to me," he said, "or how much it hurt you to break up with me."

"Come on," I said. "You knew that."

"I thought I was the only one who was hurting," he said, his long fingers nervously twirling his glass, though he did not take a sip. "Maybe you were more stoic with me then, acting kind of like the grown-up not wanting to upset the kid by being upset. And maybe I was too young and dumb to see."

He set down his glass and reached for my

hand. "I thought maybe the ending of the book, with him in Tokyo and her in New York thinking about each other, was a message to me."

"Um, no," I said. Though now that he mentioned it, maybe?

"Last time we saw each other after being apart a long time, we fell back in love," he said.

That had happened, I acknowledged.

"So I thought maybe you were trying to tell me that you wanted us to see if that could happen again."

He was still holding my hand and gazing lovingly at my face.

"Uh, no," I said, snatching my hand away. *Right?*

"*Then* you invited me to your party," he said.

"I thought it was time we were friendly."

"That's what you said last time. And half an hour later, we were tearing each other's clothes off."

I admit, I *did* want to tear his clothes off. But I also knew having sex with him could make me fall in love with him again, whether I thought it was a good idea or not. It was only by staying on this side of sex, *well* on this side of sex, that I had any hope of turning my fate around.

I'd only really loved one man in my entire life, and that was Josh. Oh, maybe I'd loved my husband back at the beginning of our relationship, but I was happier with Josh than I'd ever been with David. But Josh and I could never truly be happy together again. Therefore I had to make sure not to fall in love with him, which meant I should not have sex with him, which meant I should not be lounging on his private rooftop, drinking champagne.

I drained my glass. He still had not taken one swallow.

"I can't be the reason somebody doesn't have kids, Josh," I said.

I confess: I had rehearsed that line alone in the Maine cabin many times.

"I didn't just want kids! I wanted them with you!"

"And I didn't want them at all. You knew that. Did you think you were going to change my mind?"

"I thought we'd discuss it, and if you still felt that way, we'd go on, happy as before."

"But how could we be happy," I said, "with that between us?"

"I could have been happy," he said.

I wanted to believe that. I suppose I'd wanted to believe that all along, when I'd known deep down that the issue of children

59

must be lurking somewhere for him and that, however strenuously he denied it, it would raise its head at some point and bite me.

He moved closer to me. Put his arms around me. And then he kissed me.

It felt so good, like falling into your own bed after being on the road for months, like turning your face to the sun after a long winter in a cold house. Did I really need to leave the past behind in order to move into the future?

But no, no. Even if getting back together with Josh was what I wanted, which it wasn't (it wasn't!), doing it this way made me feel really dirty, and not in a good way.

"Josh, aren't you engaged?"

"Things aren't great between me and Zen," he mumbled.

That did not make me feel better. I had never seen Josh as a player. But if he could do it to her, couldn't he do it to me? I'd been cheated on once, by my ex-husband, and that had been devastating. It felt cosmically wrong to do that to somebody else.

"I can't get in the middle of that," I said.

He edged closer. "You were here first," he said, trying to slip his arms back around me.

I pushed him off and stepped back.

"Stop!" I said. "You've got to figure out your relationship with Zen before you try to start anything between us."

"If I break up with Zen, are you going to be there waiting?" he asked.

"I don't know, Josh," I said. "It's like with having kids. You've got to resolve this for yourself first, and then we'll see where I am."

"How was it seeing Josh?" Maggie asked.

Everybody who lived at Maggie's besides Maggie — Frankie, the kids, the nannies — had gone to bed. It was just the two of us face-to-face on the big carved-wood Indian sofas, each lounging against our personal pile of pillows. There was no place on earth I felt more comfortable.

I wanted to say it was fine, the way I'd been telling myself it would be fine, but I couldn't lie, not to Maggie.

"It was really confusing," I confessed. "I'm so attracted to him, but at the same time I don't want to get back together with him. So the whole time I was torn between wanting to jump into his arms and run away screaming."

"What do you think that's about?" Maggie asked me.

"Part of it is just that he looks so damn

61

good. The older he gets, the handsomer he looks."

"When does that stop happening for men?" Maggie asked.

"Their eighties?" I ventured with a smirk.

"Whereas women are supposed to peak in their mid-twenties and then go steadily downhill for the next sixty years."

"I definitely cannot pass for twenty-six anymore," I told Maggie.

"Oh, boo hoo. Poor baby only got to be in her twenties for two decades. Time to grow up, sweetie."

"I don't know if I even want to have a birthday party this year," I told Maggie.

"We have to have one, it's our centennial!"

Starting when we were eight and talked our mothers into throwing us a joint Sweet 16 party, Maggie and I had always celebrated our birthdays together. At fifteen, we wore tight black cocktail dresses and red lipstick to celebrate our thirtieth. When we were in college, we turned forty in our dorm room, dressed in vintage negligees and drinking chilled martinis. And we cheered ourselves up about *really* turning forty by hosting an eightieth while wearing gray wigs and adult diapers. That didn't seem so funny, now that we were about to turn a collective 100.

"Aren't you freaked out about turning fifty?" I asked her.

I certainly was. I may not have been faking my age anymore, but I was still living like a twenty-six-year-old, with no home, little savings, few responsibilities, and even less security. And a lot more fear than I'd had five years ago that I'd never be able to find those things.

"To be honest," said Maggie, "I'm happier than I've ever been. My career is more satisfying and successful, I'm having the best sex of my entire life, and I think I look better than I've ever looked — or at least I feel better about how I look."

"Well sure, I can see how you'd feel good about getting older," I said. "You're married to a wonderful person; your kids are little enough to adore you; you've got a booming career; plenty of money; a huge, beautiful home . . ."

"You could be married; you could have cute little kids," Maggie said. "You could be living in a big loft; you could be writing full-time and still have plenty of money."

"That's not true," I said, hearing the edge in my voice. "How could I have all those things?"

"You could have married Josh," Maggie said.

I took a deep breath and fell back hard against the pillows. Right: Marry Josh and go back to square one, having babies and feeling torn about how I was spending every minute of every day for the next few decades. Or marry Josh and make him sacrifice one of the deepest pleasures of life.

"I didn't want to marry Josh," I finally said.

"Exactly," said Maggie, as if that explained everything. "It was your choice, just like it was your choice to go to Maine and your choice to write a novel about being younger, and now it's your choice to be back in New York doing, I hope, exactly what you want to do."

"You make it sound like you choose everything that happens to you," I said, making no effort to hide my annoyance. "Sometimes shit just happens."

Maggie leaned eagerly forward and interrupted me. "Sure it does, but at this point you can't just let shit happen, you've got to make it happen. It's not about what you have or what you do, but whether you love your life. So, Liza, are you doing everything you can to live the life you want? And if you're not, when are you going to start?"

# SIX

Kelsey FaceTimed me a few nights later when the kids were still running around out in Maggie's loft, but I was already under the covers in my narrow bed in my tiny room, communing with my dear laptop.

I had just googled *Should you sleep with your ex?* It might not be such a bad idea, said most of the results on the first page. Now I was looking for something that would tell me why I shouldn't do it.

"I've got awesome news!" Kelsey sang.

She was walking, maybe on a beach; the camera was jerking around too much to tell for sure. Her face was in shadow, backlit by the still-bright sun, hanging low in the sky behind her. I caught flashes of palm trees.

"Tell me!" I said, already excited.

"I sold the show!"

"What?" I said, my voice rising, my heart-beat quickening. "What happened?"

"Remember Stella Power?" she said.

The name rang a bright, sparkly bell, but one that was very far away.

"Was she in that teenage movie?"

"That thriller, back in the nineties, with the guy who later played James Bond."

"Oh, right." I could picture her now, as she had looked in the airbrushed poster that my brother and many other teenage boys in America had hung on their walls. A few years younger than me, she was the most famous young woman in America for a few minutes, with her huge, wavy golden hair and her long-legged, big-boobed Barbie body. She and her handsome costar boyfriend were pictured together at the Oscars, in London, on the beach in Mexico.

"Didn't they date?"

"Back in the day. But now she's married to Barry Whipple."

"Barry Whipple?"

"The head of Whipple Studios! He's one of the most powerful men in Hollywood."

I guess I should have known that. There was a little edge to Kelsey's voice, as if she was annoyed at me for not knowing who Barry Whipple was. But Hollywood was a world to me as mysterious as British politics or Paris fashion.

"Wow. Okay," I said.

"They've been married for, like, ever, and

they have something like six children."

"Six children!"

"Some adopted, some biological, whatever. And they have this incredible *compound* in Malibu, which is where I just was, when Stella told me she wants to make *Younger.*"

"Wow, so, what does that mean?"

"It means she's going to star in it, her husband is going to finance it, and we got an order for a pilot."

"That's good, right?" I said tentatively.

Kelsey laughed. "That's as good as it gets right now: a big studio behind you, a star who wants to play the lead. . . ."

It *was* exciting. The very rhythm of Kelsey's voice was making me excited. Except I couldn't help but feel a little disappointed. "What happened to Sutton Foster?" I said.

"I know, she would have been fabulous," Kelsey said. "But we couldn't turn down this kind of package, which comes with generous financing and support from the top."

"I mean, has Stella Power done anything in the past twenty-five years?" I said. "How do we know she can even still act?"

"That is pretty ironic," said Kelsey, after a beat, "given the subject and the source."

When I'd realized what I said, I was awash

in shame.

"You're right, of course," I said. "In fact, it's perfect, because she knows the situation from the inside out. She'll be *living* it while making the show!"

"Exactly!" said Kelsey. "See, you're catching on."

"So, what happens next?" I asked.

"I write a script," Kelsey said. She had stopped walking. She was definitely at the beach, but closer to the parking lot now, with more cars and cement than sand and ocean as her backdrop.

"*You* write the script?" I said.

Kelsey had always been an editor, a producer, an adapter, but not really a writer.

"That's the way it usually works," Kelsey said. "The show creator writes the pilot script. That's literally the Guild definition."

"Could *I* write the script?" I said.

Kelsey frowned. "Writing a TV pilot script is very different from writing a novel."

"Maybe we could do it together," I said, instantly warming to the idea. "We always loved working together. This would be the perfect project for us to start again."

"I thought you didn't want to move to LA," Kelsey said.

"Why would I have to move to LA? Couldn't we just do it online?"

Kelsey was already shaking her head no. "Stella wants to be involved in the creative process," Kelsey said, making air quotes as well as a dismissive face. "She thinks it's going to be fun."

"Okay, well, we could FaceTime," I said.

"No," Kelsey said firmly.

"Can she come to New York?"

"Six kids," said Kelsey. "Plus, it's not like you have one meeting and that's it. You keep talking and talking over several days and weeks."

"How many days and weeks?" I said.

"I can't pinpoint, but probably about three or four weeks."

"Oh," I said. "I can come for three or four weeks."

"Or maybe a little longer," she said.

"How much longer? Caitlin's baby is due at the end of August, so I need to be back well before that."

"Oh," said Kelsey. "No problem. We'll be finished *shooting* before the end of August."

Shooting. That introduced another potentially disturbing problem. "Do I have to be there for the shooting?" I said.

That word didn't sound right. I felt like I was hiring a hit person. Shoot? Not really better.

"No, because we're shooting in New

69

York," Kelsey said.

"What? Are you sure Stella will agree to that?"

"It's as much of a New York story as, I don't know, *Sex and the City*. It wouldn't be practical to shoot it anywhere else."

"Okay. Phew. Great," I said. "I was worried about what would happen if it was a big hit and I had to be there all the time. Caitlin would seriously never forgive me if I moved to LA."

"If having a big hit turns out to be a problem, you'll be able to fly yourself and Caitlin and your whole family back and forth from LA to New York in your private jet," Kelsey told me.

"What?" I said. "Really?"

"Don't count the money yet," Kelsey said. "Does that mean you're going to come out here and work on it with me? Because I would love that."

"I would love that too," I said.

I told Kelsey I'd let her know my decision by Monday morning and clicked off the phone. Though the kids were still shrieking and pounding across the floor in the loft, that was no longer a distraction. I blinked at the page of search results on whether you should have sex with your ex: Why did I think the internet could help me with a

70

question I couldn't answer for myself?

I closed that window and opened a fresh document.

*Younger,* I typed at the top of the page. And below that: *Pilot.*

# SEVEN

Every Sunday evening, Maggie cooked one of her mother's secret family recipes for a rotating cast of family and friends. Since Frankie had come on the scene, a great addition had been their thematically clever cocktail of the week.

"This week's drink," said Frankie, displaying their extra-jumbo cocktail shaker to the right and then to the left in a Vanna White kind of move, "I call the Mayday. . . ."

"I think that's already a drink," said Caitlin's husband, Ravi, bouncing a basketball on the concrete floor. Ravi was a math genius — one of those freaky kids who goes to Harvard at fourteen. The year he graduated from Harvard, he grew seven inches and got drafted by the European basketball league. He saw all of Europe, played some ball, came back to go to medical school — he may have gotten a law degree in there too — and now he was a resident at Einstein. His only real fault was that he thought he was perfect.

"But *my* Mayday," said Frankie, beginning to shake the shaker, "is short for Maydaylightsavingsbank. I don't know if you've heard of it?"

Frankie rattled the cocktail shaker, now over their head. "It's got a little Russian vodka in it for May first being a celebration of revolution," they said. "It's got some brandy because that's what you drink in an emergency — mayday, get it? And then it's got some lemon juice."

"What does the lemon juice stand for?" said Caitlin, who was cradling her belly as if her hands were the only thing keeping it aloft.

"That symbolizes daylight," said Frankie, "and I hope you like that part, because yours is going to be ninety-nine percent lemon juice."

"What's the other one percent?" I asked.

My pregnant daughter grinned. "A splash of champagne."

"Do you think that's a good idea?" I said.

"I'm a doctor, and I say it's fine," said Ravi.

"I'm a cook, and I say it's time to eat," said Maggie.

Often on Sundays while Maggie cooked,

73

the rest of us played a game together — Go Fish or Mother May I — but tonight the kids were clamoring to watch a movie. Ollie made a half-hearted pitch for *How to Train Your Dragon,* but his stepsisters succeeded in overruling him in favor of *The Little Mermaid.* They tore into their parents' bedroom and soon we heard the sweet songs of "Under the Sea," with its Cole Porteresque rhymes.

"Your girls are so heteronormative," Caitlin said.

"Tell me about it," said Frankie.

"It's because of all the crap they watch," Maggie said.

"So why do you let them watch it?" Ravi asked earnestly. He took Caitlin's hand. "I mean, we're going one hundred percent screen-free, at least until the baby starts school."

"Letting them watch TV gives me time to work and have a social life," said Maggie, "so I consider it a feminist act."

Caitlin laughed. "You're such a great model of working motherhood," she said. "You had two kids in one year all by yourself, and instead of giving up your whole life, you became even *more* successful after you had kids."

My daughter might not have meant that

as a criticism of me, but I couldn't help but feel she was comparing Maggie's international success during the early years of single motherhood of near twins unfavorably with my own full-time focus on one measly kid.

"Hey, I didn't have those kids all by myself," Maggie said, jabbing her wooden spoon in Caitlin's direction. "Your mother was here with me every step of the way, and I remember you changing quite a few diapers too, Caitie."

"But then Caitlin got a nursing job and I moved to Maine," I reminded her.

"I was around by that time," said Frankie.

"And I also had plenty of help from Isabella and Graziella and Marianne and Seymour," Maggie said, referencing her most trusted childcare helpers and housekeepers.

"Seymour?" said Ravi.

"The manny," said Maggie, as if that were a standard household position.

"What did you do for childcare when you had Ollie?" Caitlin asked Frankie.

"My ex stayed home with him for the first year," said Frankie. "After we split up, I did some textbook editing from home for a while until I found a good day care situation."

"What are you going to do about work,

75

childcare, that whole thing, Caitlin?" asked Maggie.

I hadn't mentioned anything to Maggie about Caitlin wanting me to be her nanny, figuring that Maggie would be critical of Caitlin for suggesting such a thing. For underestimating my stature in the world. Maggie's kids were still young and she was still innocent: She'd find out that they wouldn't hold her in such high esteem forever.

Caitlin shot me a sharp glance. "I've been trying to look at day care centers, but most of them don't take infants, and you can't even get them to call you back," Caitlin said. "I went to this one corporate place and it was so depressing."

"I can ask my nannies if they know anyone," Maggie offered.

"I don't want someone too young," said Caitlin. "I just don't trust they'd know what to do in an emergency."

"I got an interesting call from Kelsey Friday night," I announced. "She sold the *Younger* show and she invited me to go out to LA and help her write it."

"*What?*" said Maggie. "Why didn't you tell me right away? This is huge. Congratulations."

She held up her glass in a toast, and the

76

others followed suit. All except Caitlin.

"You just got back from living on an island with no cell service for nearly two years," said Caitlin. "You don't have a place to live yet. And you're running off to California?"

"I'm not *running off,*" I said, trying to sound convinced. "It is work."

"Oh, riiiiight, *flying* off to LA, pretending that you're a screenwriter now," Caitlin said. "What's your next book going to be called — *Youngerer?*"

"That's not fair," Maggie said. "Why shouldn't your mother take this opportunity? It's her book; it's a once-in-a-lifetime chance, she's got to lean in."

"It's only for three or four weeks," I said.

"I'm only going to be pregnant for eighteen more weeks," Caitlin said. "You promised you'd be here for me."

"What do you need from your mother in the next three or four weeks that only she can give you?" Maggie asked. "Seriously, Ravi could, like, lift a car off you all by himself. I'm right here if you need money or wisdom —"

"I don't know how to make a list," said Caitlin, "but yes, there are things that only your mother can give you, no matter what age you are. Don't you feel that with your kids?"

Maggie had to acknowledge that was true, as did Frankie, after amending mother to parent.

"You're right," I said. "I'm staying in New York."

"Good choice," Frankie said to me. "New York is way better than LA."

Maggie looked taken aback. "You've never even been to LA."

"Now you know why," said Frankie.

Caitlin couldn't help breaking into a smile. "I guess that settles it," she said to me. "You're staying."

"I think you should go to LA, Liza," said Ravi.

"What?" said Caitlin, a shocked look on her face. "You're supposed to be on my side."

"I am on your side," Ravi said. "Your mother being here is causing more problems than it's solving."

"What?" I said.

"I'm sorry, Liza, but it's true. You're so worried about Caitlin all the time, like she needs you there at her elbow every second or something terrible is going to happen. . . ."

I began to explain. "I had two miscarriages—"

"We know, Liza. That must have been ter-

78

rible for you," Ravi said. "But you talking about it all the time is making Caitlin think that we're going to lose *our* baby."

I was horrified. "Is that true, Caitie?" I said.

"Kind of," she said.

"Oh God, I'm so sorry," I said. "I never meant to make you feel scared."

"Okay, well, I guess it's two to two," said Maggie. "You're the tiebreaker, Liza. What's it going to be?"

I didn't want to say no to Caitlin. But I didn't want to say no to LA because I was afraid to say no to Caitlin. The truth was, I wanted to go to LA.

"It's only a short trip," I told my daughter. "It could be great for my career, which would mean I'd have more money to help you buy a place and get a place for myself. I know you're worried about me finding more stability —"

Caitlin held up her hand. "I know you want to go, so you should just go," she said. "But don't try to make it sound like you're doing it for me."

# EIGHT

Two days later I found myself sitting on a vast white marble patio overlooking the Pacific Ocean, staring into the blue, blue eyes of actress Stella Power. Stella still looked amazingly like her poster girl self. All I could think about, smiling and nodding at her as if this were a normal conversation, was that her hair was so *thick*.

"How do you get your hair like that?" I blurted.

She laughed, exactly like Barbie might laugh if she could.

"Easy, compared with sitting around all day being a creative *genius*!" She squeezed my knee. I could just make out, on the other side of her, Kelsey rolling her eyes.

"I think the hair is harder," I said, utterly fascinated.

My own hair used to be effortlessly thick and flowing but lately had been getting so thin I was worried I'd inherited my dad's baldness gene. I'd never been much of a whiz at the beautifying arts, which had been a distinct disadvantage when I was trying to look fifteen years younger every day.

"Oh, well, some of it's extensions," she said, reaching up and fiddling around as if she were trying to tease out a nit, and instead removed a huge hank of hair. I nearly screamed. "And then I had stem cells injected into my scalp to stimulate hair growth. It's amazing."

I told Stella I'd never heard of such a thing. "It's still experimental," she said, "but Barry is a big donor to the medical school, so I got into a clinical trial. The really beautiful thing is that they get the stem cells from your *fat,* so you get a little lipo in the bargain."

I told Stella that I couldn't imagine where they found any fat on her body.

"Stop, I'm like eighteen percent body fat!" Stella said.

"You look amazing," I told her sincerely. "You really do look twenty-six."

As someone who knew from the inside out how difficult it was to achieve this, I was in awe.

"Good surgery," she responded, as if that were as natural as good diet or good genes.

"You mean, plastic surgery?" I said.

81

"What else?" said Stella. "I've already had my whole face done once and my neck done twice. Nose, of course. Pussy, of course of course, after pushing out all those kids. Boobs, though then I had them undone because Barry thought they were too big."

"That must have . . . hurt," I said.

"Love is pain!" said Stella. "You know Barry, don't you, Kelsey?"

"Not yet," Kelsey said.

Stella cupped her hands around her mouth and called, "Barry, Bar!"

A gnomish white-haired man walking along a dark hedge of cypress trees at the far side of the property gave us a wave without actually looking our way. He was dressed in a khaki jumpsuit and was engaged in an animated conversation, seemingly with himself. I had assumed he was the gardener, or at least one of them.

Stella motioned to him. "Come over and meet the *Younger* ladies!" she called.

He smiled and waved again but kept on walking.

"Now my boobs could turn purple and he wouldn't notice," Stella said. "What did you have done before your little *Younger* stunt?"

"You mean, done as in plastic surgery?" I said. "Nothing."

"Now *that* is amazing," she said. "Though

this was a while ago, right?"

"Five years," I said.

Stella sighed deeply. "I wish *I* was a New York intellectual and never had to worry about how I looked."

I barely had time to consider whether that insult had been deliberate when out from the house hurtled a small blond child, screaming and running straight for the swimming pool. I was about to leap up and run after him when a young man appeared on his heels, making play dinosaur sounds. The child screamed louder and ducked into a structure covered with gauzy white fabric beside the swimming pool.

"Brooksy, be careful with the massage tent!" Stella called. And then to us, "One of the kids knocks it down every single week."

Brooks tore out the other end of the tent and hurled himself into the pool, his caregiver right behind him.

"Brooks is my youngest, and I was so devastated when it was time for him to start school, I decided to homeschool all six of the children."

I was astonished. "Isn't that a lot of work?"

"Oh God, yes," Stella said. "It takes ten teachers."

Stella tucked her feet up and lifted her arms to twist her thick mane of hair into a knot on top of her head. The minute she dropped her arms, it cascaded back around her shoulders.

"I don't know about you ladies," Stella said. "But I'm ready for a little wake and bake."

She extracted a white vape pen from the folds of her silk blouse and took a deep draw, holding her breath while extending the pen to me.

It actually took me an embarrassingly long time to realize she was offering me marijuana. I was shocked, until I remembered that I was in California now. It was legal.

"I'm flattered you've mistaken me for the kind of person who smokes pot at eleven in the morning," I said. "But, well, no."

Stella raised her eyebrows, but instead of saying anything, offered the pen to Kelsey, who also shook her head no.

"Are you guys sober?" said Stella. "That's cool. I mean, I've been sober lots of times."

"I've never been sober," I said.

"I'm sober curious," said Kelsey.

"Does that include 'shrooms?" said Stella, mint-sized puffs of smoke escaping from her mouth.

"I would guess so?" said Kelsey.

"I've never tried mushrooms," I said. "Or any hallucinogenic."

84

I felt like a missionary.

"It's a religious experience," said Stella, finally expelling a cloud of vapor. "Anyway, I had a vision of this enormous white bird —"

Two little girls in bathing suits ran screaming out of the house, one shooting the other with a bazooka-sized water gun. A middle-aged woman with dark hair that dangled down past her waist trailed after them, saying something that no one was listening to, not even a little bit.

"Talullah!" Stella broke in. "Do not shoot Djuna with that gun. We have talked about nonviolence. Marisol, donde did they get that, how do you say *machine gun* in Spanish?"

Marisol said, "Mr. Tane give it to them."

"I will talk to Mr. Tane," Stella said. She stood up, and Kelsey and I followed suit, as you might with royalty.

"Tane is our massage therapist," Stella explained. I thought she might be saying Donny, or Tawny. "Also our surfing instructor, yoga master, martial arts teacher for the boys — well, you know, the girls too, theoretically. And he's a gun enthusiast! I tell him, you can't bring those things near me and the kids, but look what he does." She shook her head, smiling fondly as if discuss-

85

ing one of her children. "Things are different in Samoa, or wherever it is he's from."

A young woman dressed in white emerged from the house. "Can we talk about lunch?" she asked.

Stella grimaced and shook her hands at the heavens. "I'm working, people, working!" she shouted. "You're all going to have to start figuring things out for yourselves. Come on, ladies, we'll take this meeting down to the beach."

Stella took off across the lawn, Kelsey and I scrambling to catch up. She had the supernatural ability to walk faster than either of us could run. She finally stopped outside a little white-painted wooden structure that looked like a place where ponies might live. Magical ponies. She pulled open the old-fashioned barn-style double doors to reveal a garage filled with golf carts, along with surfboards, boogie boards, wet suits, paddle boards, and windsurfing equipment.

"Do either of you surf?" she said. "If Tane's down there, he can give you a lesson."

Another thing I wished I could say yes to.

"Another time," said Kelsey. "We're looking forward to hearing your thoughts on the pilot so we can start writing."

"Right, right, we're business ladies," said

Stella. "Wait there."

She disappeared into the shed and a minute later backed out behind the wheel of a whirring golf cart. Kelsey and I climbed onto the back, hanging on tight as Stella took off, bouncing over the lawn toward the ocean. It was a good thing I wasn't looking forward, so I couldn't see the sheer cliff down to the water come into view, or Stella stop within six inches of it.

Walling off the cliff was a weathered wooden gate, locked with a keypad. Stella's fingers danced over the numbers until the gate popped open. She led us down a long wooden staircase to a beach that stretched empty in both directions as far as we could see.

"Is all this your private beach?" I asked, astonished. Beaches weren't this empty anywhere on the East Coast, even Maine.

"God, no," Stella said dismissively. "We share it with at least four other families."

The wind off the water was brisk and cool and the beach was in shadow, given that the morning sun was still in the east, behind the mountains. I'd watched it come up this morning, thought of Caitlin going about her day, took a picture of the sunrise and considered sending it to her, but resisted.

Stella took out her vape pen and sucked on it as we walked down the beach. She offered it first to Kelsey, who was walking on the land side of her, but again Kelsey shook her head no. Then she offered it to me. I had scored the water side and was relishing the feel of my toes in the icy Pacific Ocean. I took the vape pen. I'd smoked occasionally these past years with Josh and with Maggie, but not since I'd moved to Maine. The weed hit me fast and hard; within seconds, I was not sure I'd be able to speak cogently.

"Back to my big white bird," Stella said. "I saw this bird, and I asked him what he thought about *Younger,* and he said he thought the boss should be a man instead of a woman. Isn't that crazy?"

"Totally crazy," I said.

"But interesting," said Kelsey.

"I was thinking," said Stella, "that maybe instead of a younger guy, Liza could go out with an *older* guy."

"Alice," I said.

"What?"

"The character's name is Alice."

Stella laughed. "Yeah, but I like the name Liza so much better. What if, I don't know, she's this woman pretending to be younger, who goes to work for this guy who thinks

88

he's too old for her, except they're really the same age?"

"That's interesting," said Kelsey.

"But so not this story," I said.

Stella stopped and looked out to the horizon, as if searching for a ship. "I think maybe the character, Liza, Alice, whatever, should be younger in the show."

"*Actually* younger?" I said. I really wished I had not smoked that weed. Nothing was making sense.

"Yes, *actually* thirty-five-ish, playing twenty-two-ish." She said *actually* as if I'd pronounced it like Dame Maggie Smith.

"Her daughter is supposed to be in college," I pointed out. "Are we saying she was a teen mom?"

"So we'll make the kid younger. Or get rid of the kid!"

"We can't get rid of the kid," I said. I couldn't let myself imagine that, even in fiction.

"Kids can be a pain on the set," said Kelsey.

"You know what it's like, you're a pro," said Stella to Kelsey. "I think if she were pretending to be twenty-two and her boss is fiftyish —"

"You said she and the boss were really the same age," I said. "Did you mean they're both fifty or both thirty-five?"

"I didn't mean the *same* same age," Stella said. "I guess I have to be careful about my language around writers."

"I know what you're trying to say," said Kelsey.

That was good, because I had no fucking clue.

"I can get Hugo Fielding to play the boss slash older boyfriend," said Stella.

"Hugo Fielding, your actual old boyfriend?" I said, astonished. "I can't believe you two stayed friends."

Their love affair had ended disastrously and publicly when Hugo left her for Madonna. I still remembered the *People* magazine cover featuring Stella's tear-streaked face.

"Hugo stays friends with *all* his old girlfriends," Stella said. "He is the sweetest, most thoughtful, most generous guy on earth."

"Really?" I said. I couldn't imagine talking about any of my exes, even Josh, in such glowing terms. "We're both talking about 007 Hugo Fielding, right?"

"He's a total doll," Stella said. "But don't mention 007 to him. He's trying to transcend that role."

"It would be *amazing* to have Hugo Field-

90

ing in the show," said Kelsey.

"You really think so?" I said. "That doesn't make any sense to me. The guy needs to be younger."

"Tane!" Stella waved excitedly. It was only then that I noticed the large dark man sitting astride a surfboard beyond the break line, bobbing in the waves. Between the long black hair plastered to his head, his wetsuit the same oily-looking dark color as the water, and the shade that still covered the coastline and the beach, he was nearly invisible despite his prodigious size.

"I've got to talk to you!" Stella called. Oh, right, the toy gun.

She ran into the surf up to her knees, still waving her arms as if she were drowning. He hopped to a crouch on the board with the agility of a frog, looked back over his shoulder, and as a massive wave built behind him, took off flying toward shore. Stella, laughing, waded out to meet him. Just this side of the breakers, he hopped off his board, Stella grabbed the other side of it, and they headed back into the surf, talking animatedly across the board as if it were a café table. They paused to duck beneath the huge waves that crashed over their heads, resurfacing each time farther out in the sea. Kelsey and I stood there with smiles

91

plastered on our faces as if we expected that any second Stella would return and resume our discussion. But instead, Tane — so muscled you could see every bulge clearly through his wetsuit — held the board steady while Stella hoisted herself up onto it. Then she stretched out flat and began paddling as he pushed and kicked from behind.

"Are we supposed to keep standing here?" I said.

"I have no fucking idea," said Kelsey.

"Are you mad about something?"

Kelsey, grim-faced, stared straight ahead.

"I hope this doesn't mean the whole thing is over before it even began," she said finally.

"What are you talking about?" I said.

Instead of answering, Kelsey kept her eyes trained on the ocean. Stella was now sitting on the board, her white silk shirt so drenched it was nearly transparent. I waved. Stella did not wave back or even glance our way.

"Maybe she had a surfing lesson scheduled," I said.

"Maybe she's never going to talk to us again," Kelsey said.

Kelsey turned and walked away down the sand so fast it took me a minute to register that she was leaving. I had to run to catch up with her.

"I don't get it," I said to Kelsey. "What's happening?"

But she just kept walking with her mouth set in that grim, tight line. I seemed to have already screwed up my life in LA, and I hadn't even been here twenty-four hours.

# NINE

"Why didn't she just disagree?" I said.

We were sitting in Kelsey's living room facing each other, our feet up on the carved wooden coffee table. There were walls of glass on opposite sides of the room, one looking out over the city skyline and the other facing blue mountain peaks. Kelsey's New York apartment had had a traditional look, filled with beige damask furniture bought when she planned to marry her banker boyfriend, Thad. That was all gone, replaced with spare pieces in white and black and gray, more architectural than comfortable. With her move to LA, her home seemed to have acquired a more casual style and sleeker bones, much like Kelsey herself.

"Celebrities don't like to say anything directly," Kelsey informed me. "They have people to do that for them."

Kelsey's hand rested on her dog, Theo —

a wheaten terrier: more elegant than a Lab, sturdier than a poodle — who was curled up on the sofa beside her. Theo's hair was the same shade of blond as Kelsey's own.

"I couldn't just stand there and let her change all my characters and my story," I said. "She wanted to get rid of Josh, and Caitlin, and Mrs. Whitney, all in one stroke!"

"It was a conversation," Kelsey said. "You let her talk and do not confront."

"You made it sound like you agreed with everything she said," I told Kelsey. "You totally threw me under the bus."

"That wasn't throwing you under the bus, that was diplomacy," Kelsey said. "Things work differently out here. The TV business is not like the book business."

"What's it like, then?" I asked, in genuine innocence.

"There is a lot more money on the table and a lot more people are involved," she said. "It's higher stakes, which means there's a lot more competition and a much bigger emphasis on doing what you need to do to attract viewers."

"This isn't about attracting viewers," I said. "It's about making Stella happy!"

"And making Stella happy means making the network happy means us getting more support and more money to turn this into a successful series," Kelsey said. "Isn't that what you want?"

"Yes," I said. "But I don't want to completely abandon my own story."

"You see, that's what I'm confused about: Is it your story or isn't it?" Kelsey said, uncrossing her feet, then crossing them again. "If it is, then yes, what matters most is the truth and keeping the story as close as possible to the facts."

"I didn't mean my story, as in my personal story," I said. "I meant my story as in my novel."

"So it's fiction," said Kelsey.

"Officially, it's fiction," I agreed.

"But you see, that's the issue," Kelsey said, setting her feet on the floor and leaning forward. "If this is fiction, if this is not your story but just a story, then you've got to sacrifice real people and events in the service of making the best possible show. Are you willing to do that?"

"I want to make a good show too," I said, refusing to give her a direct answer. Because really, she knew there *was* no direct answer. My story wasn't black or white, fact or fiction, truth or lies. It was both, and I wanted it all: fidelity to my deeper story, while preserving complete deniability. "I just don't see how making the boyfriend older improves the story."

"Hugo Fielding can make the show a hit," Kelsey said.

I shook my head. Who was my character Alice, what was *Younger* even about without Josh and Mrs. Whitney? Maybe they could change all these details and turn it into a better story than the book I wrote, but did I want to be part of that? Part of me wanted to get up and go back home. But if I abandoned this project, was anyone going to stand up for my book at all?

"You might be right about that," I said, trying to be conciliatory without sacrificing any ground.

"Listen, I want to stay true to your story and also make an amazing TV show," Kelsey said. "Can you trust me to find a way to accomplish both those things?"

"That's what I want too," I said, relieved that we seemed to be back on the same page.

"You know the book about writing *Bird by Bird*?" said Kelsey. Every writer and person who worked with writers knew that winsome guidebook by Anne Lamott, who deconstructed the writing process and advised would-be authors to approach their writing one small step at a time: bird by bird. "Well, in the TV business, that might be called *Meeting by Meeting.*"

"What does that mean?" I said.

"It means before we make any decisions, the next step is to meet Hugo Fielding."

I had to admit, as ruffled as my feathers were about this whole older man idea, I was intrigued to meet Hugo Fielding, whom I had always found more attractive than I wanted to admit. *Is that a gun in your pocket, James Bond, or are you just looking to fuck me?*

I said that I supposed, if I really had to, I'd be open to meeting one of the world's most famous and attractive movie stars. One meeting, and we'd take it from there.

I spotted Hugo Fielding instantly, sitting with Stella in the corner booth at the back of the Warner Brothers dining room. Living in New York, I'd seen a lot of celebrities. Some of them — Daniel Day Lewis, Reese Witherspoon — could make themselves look anonymous enough to blend into any crowd. Others — Bill Clinton, Diane Keaton — were magnetic before you even registered their identity.

Hugo Fielding was that kind of star.

For all the complaining I'd done about meeting Hugo Fielding, my heart began to beat faster and I felt fluttering in my stomach. This guy was a bona fide celebrity, and meeting him was like walking into a movie. I'd been stunned when Maggie started screaming after I told her I was meeting him.

"I love him," she said. "I even told Frankie, he's my celebrity pass."

"How could I not know this?"

"Shame," Maggie said. "I've only wanted to fuck one cis man in my entire life, and he's the same cis man who every basic bitch wants to fuck."

Hugo unfolded himself from the booth, even taller and slimmer than he looked on-screen, or in my imagination. Kelsey and I were both wearing high-heeled boots, Kelsey's paired with a vegan leather miniskirt while I was rocking my standard black go-to-meeting pants. Stella was dolled up in a white silk romper, but Hugo had tossed on a worn gray tee shirt and jeans. On-screen, he had a tough, macho quality, but in person his skin was as soft and pink as if he'd just come from a facial, and he seemed almost slight despite his height and his broad shoulders. His hair was boyishly thick, flecked with gray hairs at such perfect intervals they might have been hand-placed.

"I am so excited to meet you," he said,

shaking Kelsey's hand. "I was a huge fan of your *Jane Eyre.*"

He inclined himself toward her as he spoke, so they were eye-to-eye.

"You watched *Jane Eyre*?" Kelsey said. She was trying to act cool and in charge, but I'd known her long enough to tell she was flustered.

"Of course. It's my favorite book," Hugo said.

Then he turned to me and enfolded my outstretched hand in both of his.

"I can't believe I'm meeting the author of *Younger,*" he said. "I'm just . . . starstruck."

His cheeks grew even pinker as he said this, and his hands felt warmer around mine. Or maybe my hands were getting warmer all on their own.

"I'm the one who's starstruck," I admitted.

"I'm in love with your book," he said warmly. He was looking at me in wonder as if I were some magical creature, a sparkly unicorn that he'd never encountered before, yet had been waiting his whole life to find. He had twinkling brown eyes and was looking at me as if we'd just shared the best private joke. "I finished it at three in the morning. My second read, I mean. I feel like I've been living inside your head."

He chuckled and cast his eyes down, as if he were a bashful fan and I was the celebrity. This guy could not possibly be for real.

But it was hard to hang on to my cynicism given that my arm, the one attached to the hand he'd been holding, had started tingling and vibrating, as if I'd had an orgasm. Hell, maybe I was still having one.

I yanked my hand away and rubbed it as if it had been scorched.

*I will not be attracted to Hugo Fielding, I will not be attracted to Hugo Fielding, I will not be attracted to Hugo Fielding.*

Stella was wedged into the corner of the booth. Kelsey slid in beside her on the short end, while Hugo resumed his place on her other side. The only spot for me to sit was beside him.

"So, ladies," Stella said when we were all settled. "Wasn't I right? Isn't Hugo amaaaaazing?"

Hugo, who was of course sitting right there, said, "Now Stella, darling. What are they supposed to say to that?"

"Of course we think you're great," Kelsey said. "We are so thrilled that you're considering doing our show."

Hugo smiled, then turned to me. I smiled back, mainly to keep my lips from moving.

"I'm afraid you're not going to think I'm

very amazing," he said, "when I tell you I have to pass on taking a role in *Younger.*"

My heart swelled in relief and at the same time sank in disappointment. Was it possible to feel like you'd won and lost at the same time?

"Hugo!" Stella said. This obviously came as a surprise to her. "I can't accept your rejection."

"No no no, it's not a *rejection,*" he said. The native British accent he used in only some of his film roles grew stronger as his voice became more excited. "It's exactly *because* I love the book so much that I've got to turn it down."

He focused on me.

"I think it's a mistake to replace Josh, the younger guy, with an older man," he told me almost mournfully. "This is a meditation on age in America, so thematically it feels very wrong."

"Thank you," I said. I was about to add that I agreed with him, but I was aware of Kelsey's eyes on me across the table and thought I'd better leave it at that.

"Also, I could never forgive myself for replacing Mrs. Whitney," he said. "I am *totally* in love with that character."

I smiled. "I'm sure she'll be thrilled to hear that," I told him.

"So there's a *real* Mrs. Whitney?" he said.

"She owns the company that published this book. Using her real name was a little inside joke. She loved it."

"I regret that I won't get to meet her," Hugo said. "A woman who started a company when she did and still runs it, that's an amazing person. You must love working with her."

"I do," I said.

He leaned back in his seat and addressed the table. "I can't bear to think of her character not being in the show," Hugo said. "I'd hate myself if I replaced her."

"What if you didn't replace her? What if you were both there?" Kelsey said.

"Maybe she and I work shoulder to shoulder, running the company together," Hugo said, considering. "Though frankly, I don't think the book needs another character. It's perfect the way it is."

"TV soaks up a lot of story," Kelsey said, growing animated. "What if we added an older man character and *kept* the Josh character? That would add a romantic-triangle element, which viewers love."

"Hugo can't share top billing," Stella said. "He'd clearly have the bigger role and be the star." She waited a beat before adding, "I mean, the *male* star."

Hugo laughed and patted her shoulder fondly. "There's only one star of this show," he said, "and only one author of the book. Liza's the one who created these characters and this world. It's ultimately her decision whether we kill off some characters and stick in new ones."

"It's hard for me to see it any way other than the way it happened," I admitted, "which is that I was with a younger guy who actually was named Josh. He played a big part in my not just looking like a younger person but living a younger life."

"That's what I suspected," said Hugo. "I have to know: Did you and Josh end up getting back together when he came home from Japan?"

I was genuinely impressed that he'd read the book carefully enough to not only remember that detail but also have such well-formed opinions about the characters and the plot.

"Several months later, yeah," I said. "We lived together for two years, but we're not together now."

"I'm sorry to hear that," Hugo said. "It seemed like, at a very deep level, that relationship went way beyond age. Alice and Josh were perfect for each other."

"But it was age that ultimately broke us

up," I admitted. "I wouldn't date a younger man again."

"See, that's why you have to be in it, so Liza can end up with you," said Stella, slapping Hugo's arm the way eight-year-old girls hit boys they like.

"Alice," I said.

Everyone stared at me.

"The character's name is Alice," I clarified.

"Maybe I'll just call her Aliza," said Stella, giggling. "Come on, Hugo, you've got to do it."

Hugo did not look at Stella but was totally focused on me. Somehow, he'd shifted me back along the banquette so that he and I were sitting separately from Stella and Kelsey. He was leaning toward me. It was all I could do to keep myself from meeting him halfway.

"Perhaps you and I should get together, Liza," he said, "and see if we can come up with an idea that excites us both."

"That's a great idea," said Kelsey.

"That might work," I said.

*I will not have sex with Hugo Fielding, I will not have sex with Hugo Fielding, I will not have sex with Hugo Fielding.*

"Hey, I don't want to be left out of all the fun," Stella said.

"I'd like to be in on those discussions too," said Kelsey. "Maybe we can all meet at Whipple Studios."

"This is just between me and Liza," Hugo said. He wasn't touching me, but he was so close I could feel the heat of his skin. "If we talk and Liza wants me in the show, I'll do it."

By the time we made it back from lunch, it was after office hours in New York. I retreated to the guesthouse and FaceTimed Maggie. I caught her with Caitlin, walking down a city street that looked bleak and unfamiliar.

"Where are you guys?" I asked.

"Some neighborhood in Brooklyn that's not on any maps," Maggie said.

"Thrillist says it's one of the ten neighborhoods ready to pop," said Caitlin. "You can still get a house here for under two million."

Maggie jumped and clutched her hand to her throat.

"Is that a rat?" she said.

"What are you doing there?" I asked.

"Looking at a house," said Caitlin. "I think we turn left here."

"Where's Ravi?" I said.

As if Ravi could ward off the rats.

"Working, of course," said Caitlin. "And

106

I'm working all kinds of crazy hours, so I have to take advantage of free time when I get it."

"Let's cross to the other side," said Maggie. "I don't like the look of those guys."

I willed my breathing and my blood pressure to stay calm.

"How's the script coming?" asked Caitlin.

I couldn't tell her that not only hadn't we started writing the script, but we hadn't yet decided who the characters were going to be and that even Caitlin's fictional existence was suddenly up in the air.

"Interesting," I said, fully aware that as an answer it did not really make sense. "So today we had lunch with Hugo Fielding."

Maggie let out a scream, then waved her hand apologetically.

"Sorry, Officer," she called. "I'm fine. So what was he like?"

"Nice," I said. "Not what I expected."

"Who's Hugo Fielding?" said Caitlin.

"He's that gorgeous British dude who starred in all the romantic comedies back in the nineties," Maggie informed her. "He dated Meg Ryan, Renée Zellweger . . ."

"How old is this guy?" said Caitlin.

"A little older than me," I said. "I'm sure you'd recognize him."

"So you're there hanging out with movie

stars?" Caitlin asked. "I thought it was nonstop work work work."

"It is, but it turns out television work involves a lot of hanging out," I said. "I'll be back in two or three more weeks at the most."

"You've already been there two weeks," said Caitlin.

She was noticeably bigger in just those few weeks, and seemed to be walking more unsteadily. But I reminded myself that worrying about her out loud was not helpful.

"Will you still be in LA when I go out for my Hauser and Wirth opening?" said Maggie.

That was her first major West Coast art show, on the twenty-fifth, I remembered. Although it had been in my calendar forever, I'd never expected I would actually be able to attend.

"I might be," I admitted.

"If you are, will you introduce me to Hugo Fielding?"

"I'll see," I said.

"I miss you, Mom," said my daughter.

"Me too, sweetheart," I said.

I wished I were the one walking down the street in New York with my daughter, watching her belly grow bigger and taking every step of this journey to motherhood by her side. On the other hand, I was so excited to be in LA, learning about the TV business, meeting Hugo and even Stella and getting a glimpse into Kelsey's world.

It still felt exactly as it had when Caitlin was small and I had wanted to go back to work but I also had wanted to be with her. Both parts of my life exerted such powerful pulls, yet every choice required a serious sacrifice. You couldn't get anything without giving up a lot, which meant that all pleasure was underscored by pain.

This was the first time, I realized, that I'd made my Sophie's choice in favor of myself rather than my child, that I'd picked what I wanted over what my daughter wanted. I thought back to the talk Maggie and I had after I'd seen Josh, about her telling me I had to start living the life I wanted and that if I didn't, I had only myself to blame. I'd come to California because I wanted to. Now I owed it to myself, and to Caitlin too, to own my choice and make the most of being here. Living in ambivalence, dwelling on the loss, not only undercut but dishonored the gain.

# TEN

Hugo texted me an invitation to meet and talk about the show at his house in Rustic Canyon.

"Where's Rustic Canyon?" I asked Kelsey.

"Santa Monica. It's in the hills, but by the beach. It's where rich people go when they don't want anyone to find them. What's in Rustic Canyon?"

"Hugo Fielding."

"Do *not* go to Hugo Fielding's house," Kelsey said. "You don't want to get into a position where this could be mistaken for a date. It would be unprofessional, given that we're talking about working together."

"James Bond is not interested in dating me."

"He's dated every woman he's ever worked with!" she said. "*Never* date an actor. They're *professional* fakes."

At Kelsey's suggestion, instead of meeting Hugo at his house, I made a reservation for

110

lunch at the Beverly Hills Hotel. I wore jeans, sandals, and a crisp white shirt, remembering how casually Hugo had dressed when we'd met at the studio dining room. But following the maître d' around the gorgeous patio, lush with bougainvillea and dotted with round metal tables laid with formal white cloths, I felt under-dressed. It wasn't that my clothes were too informal, but that they simply didn't feel as *good* as what everybody else seemed to be wearing: They were too tight, too loose, too faded, too bright, too old, too new, too *me*. Would I ever be mature enough to feel comfortable in my own skin?

Hugo was not on the patio, and I was about to sit down to wait when the maître d' asked me to describe the person I was meeting.

"Ah," he said, when I told him it was Hugo. "Follow me."

He led me back inside, where I found Hugo seated in a dark round booth in a far corner.

"I thought we'd sit outside," I said. "It's so bright out there."

I hesitated. "The weather is gorgeous."

"The weather here is always gorgeous," he said.

I kept hesitating. The maître d' had vanished. It wasn't being inside that bothered me so much as sitting next to him in that intimate, shadowy booth.

"I thought we were here to talk about the show," I said.

"And your book," he said. "I think we'll be more comfortable in here."

I finally relented, but instead of sliding into the booth, I took the chair on the outside of the table, facing him.

He leaned toward me, hands clasped on the shiny wood, smile on his face. "I'm so curious what it was like for you pretending to be a different person," he said. "I mean, we do it on set, but that's a controlled environment and we have a script, we're playing a character. How did you pull it off twenty-four seven in your real life?"

"It wasn't twenty-four seven," I said. "I was living with my friend Maggie then, and she always knew who I really was. And I wasn't pretending to be a different person, I was just pretending to be younger."

Suddenly there was a young woman at our table, someone who, judging from her outfit, had been working behind the bar.

"I could get fired for this," she said, sotto voce, "but it's my mom's birthday and you are her absolute favorite and she would just die if I could take a picture with you."

112

"Let's FaceTime her," Hugo said.

"Seriously?"

"Yeah, scoot in. What's her name?"

I'd expected him to be a little churlish, given that Mom was the fan, not the hot bartender, but if that was true, he didn't show it at all. He took the phone, and when Mom answered, he said, "Hey, Debbie, it's Hugo. I wanted to call and say happy birthday."

There was squealing and oh-my-Godding as Hugo and the bartender both assured Debbie that this was real. When the maître d' came over to intervene, Hugo said the whole thing was his idea.

"That kind of thing happen a lot?" I asked when we were alone again.

He shrugged. "It's sweet, really, for people to care enough to connect with you. It seems kind of affected to act like you don't want to be recognized. I mean, then why did you become a movie star?"

He paused. He apparently hadn't shaved that morning; his stubble was so thick.

"That said," he continued, "if you want to get some actual work done, it is sometimes more comfortable to meet at my house. Thus the initial invitation. And my vampire-like refusal to sit on the patio."

I laughed. "I'm sorry, I didn't understand.

113

I've never had that problem."

"No, you've always been free to be yourself," he said. He sat there for a long minute then, just looking at me. I knew that look; most women did. It was the look of a boy who liked a girl.

"Tell me this," he said, still looking at me fondly, "when you were pretending to be young, did you sometimes forget and genuinely *feel* young?"

I flashed instantly on Josh, the man who mistook me for younger, who sparked the whole idea of my faking my age.

But the thing was, Josh's feelings for me weren't fake. He genuinely saw me as someone his age. And that more than anything else was what I got from him. What I craved. That feeling of being seen and admired and accepted as someone young. Because then, I truly felt young.

"With Josh," I said. "And with Kelsey, too, at the beginning. They accepted me as young, which made them treat me as young, which made me feel young, really young, all the good stuff and the bad stuff too."

"I used to feel that way when I dated younger women," he said. "It wasn't about *them* being young. It was about them making *me* feel young. If they liked me, that must mean I was as youthful and attractive

114

as they were."

It was like a piano fell on my chest. That was exactly it. Why I'd been so compelled to flirt with Josh, to lead him on, while at the same time holding back. If he liked me, if he admired me, if he wanted me again, that meant I still looked young; I could still *live* as young as I had before. I could still pretend the fiction was real.

"But you don't feel that way anymore?" I said to Hugo.

"One night I was sitting in a booth with one of them, having a great time, and then I caught sight of myself purely by accident in the mirror, and I was horrified. It was like *Beauty and the Beast.* I realized how much I'd been deluding myself, and how out of touch I was with my own life."

"You got all that from one glance in the mirror?"

"Come here," he said, gesturing for me to join him in the booth.

I slid in beside him on the round red leather bench. He pointed at the wall.

"Look in there," he said. "What do you see?"

The wall had been at my back before, but even if I had been looking straight at it, I might not have noticed that it was a mirror. Black streaked gold, it seemed at first only

115

to be as reflective as a slick of oil, but then as your eyes adjusted, you could see that it was more like a lake, the water so deep it appeared black. Hugo and I were reflected there like two ghostly figures, apparitions.

"It's us," I said.

"That's right, us," he agreed. "That's what I expected to see that night when I was out with her, two people who looked like they belonged together. Like you and me."

I felt my cheeks go warm at hearing him say that he and I looked like we belonged together, but instead of responding, I moved back to my chair on the other side of the table. "And instead you saw . . ."

"A young woman and someone who could be her father," he said. "I saw who I really was, and that was someone I didn't want to be."

When I got home, Kelsey was floating on a giant inflatable swan in the pool, wearing round pink sunglasses and a straw hat as big as an umbrella.

"How was it?" she called excitedly.

"Great," I said, but kept on walking. I knew she was dying to hear all about my meeting with Hugo and what I'd decided about making him a character in the show.

But I hadn't decided. And I couldn't

decide until I'd talked to Josh.

I retreated into the guesthouse and firmly shut the door behind me. The sprawling, low, built-in bed, which looked like something Warren Beatty might have cavorted on in the seventies, was the only place to sit, so I propped myself up against a wall of pillows and FaceTimed Josh. He answered right away, an uncertain smile on his face, as if he was happy to hear from me, but was afraid I was calling with bad news.

"I'm sorry I didn't let you know I was leaving," I said.

He exhaled, relieved that I hadn't said, *I hate you and I never want to see you again.* Behind him, through one of his office's enormous arched windows, the sun was setting over the harbor.

"No worries," he said. "Frankie filled me in."

"About the TV version of *Younger*?"

"Yeah, I heard. That's really exciting."

"I'm glad you think so." I took a breath. "There are changes some people want to make in the show."

"Changes?" he said, on alert again. "What kind of changes?"

"The star who's playing the lead — you know, me — wants us to hire her old boyfriend to play, well, her old boyfriend. Old as in aged. She thinks if she's in the show with a younger actor that he's going to look better than her."

Hugo had explained this to me at lunch. Stella wanted to avoid the *Beauty and the Beast* experience on national television.

"So Josh is going to be . . . old?" young Josh, *real* Josh said.

That *was* an idea. But probably not the right one.

"No, the guy is probably going to be a whole different character," I said.

"So what happens to Josh?" he said. "I mean, TV Josh."

"I'm not sure," I said. "I'm afraid there might not be a Josh." I couldn't help wincing. "I'm sorry."

Josh laughed. "That's okay. I'm actually relieved. Ever since Frankie told me about the show, I've been thinking it would be weird seeing a character with my name looking and acting like me on TV. But I didn't want to screw things up for you."

"So you'd rather there weren't a Josh in the show?" I said.

"I guess that's what I'm saying."

That should have been good news, but instead it stung.

"I was actually hoping to keep Josh in the show," I said. "Alice's relationship with Josh is what the whole story is about."

"Not the whole story," said Josh. "It's only part of the story. It's also about her at work, and with her friends and daughter."

I hesitated. I couldn't decide if he was downplaying his role to reassure me that he was okay with being dumped from the show, or if he really underestimated how important he'd been to me.

"Josh, it was you who made me see myself as younger, who made me believe in myself as younger," I said. "That transformation was more about how you made me feel inside, what you made me believe I could do, than it was about how I looked."

"I do see you like that," he said.

"But I'm not that person," I said. "I wasn't then, and I'm really not now. And you seeing me like that . . . It felt so good. It *feels* so good. But it's also a problem."

"You were right that I shouldn't have come on to you when I'm still with Zen."

"That's not the problem I'm talking about," I told him. "I'm talking about how I was using you. I wanted you to be attracted to me so I could feel young again."

"I *am* attracted to you," he said. "It's not about how old you look."

"It's about how old I *am*," I said. "I've always said that age didn't matter when it came to us, but I see now that it did matter. It was everything."

I'd loved Josh back then, I understood now, not despite his youth but because of it, because of how it made me feel — like I was young too. He'd made me feel like someone who I wasn't, like the pretense was real, and I wanted him to make me feel like that again. But it was time for me to let go of the fiction and live as my real self. Perhaps rewriting my story would help me rewrite my life.

It was nearly sunset, the first time since early morning that it was bearable in the hot sun to hike in Griffith Park. Though the trailheads started at the end of the neighborhood right up the hill from Kelsey's house, we drove to get there, Theo perched obediently in the backseat of Kelsey's robin's-egg blue Mini.

Hiking in the park was Kelsey's favorite thing to do in LA, and it was rapidly turning into mine too. It seemed so crazy to a New Yorker that not only was there a massive wild and wooded park a couple of miles from Hollywood and Vine, but that serious hiking up its switch-backing trails was the favorite avocation of many Angelenos. You saw everyone in the park, from impossibly

120

buff actors running straight uphill to octoge-
narians walking their dogs to groups of
Japanese tourists and multigenerational
families making a day of it. While there were
a few roads that let you drive through the
park, there were too many trails to count:
wide as a boulevard and narrow as a cat-
walk, paved and dirt, steep and flat. They
crisscrossed each other so that there were
dozens of ways to get anywhere — the
Observatory was the prime destination —
or nowhere at all. Kelsey seemed to know
every one of them, so I blindly followed
wherever she led. She said she did her best
thinking here, which made a hike in the park
the perfect venue for us to wrestle with
Hugo's potential character in *Younger.*

"I'm ready to let go of the story of the
older woman falling in love with the younger
guy," I told Kelsey.

She smiled but raised her eyebrows at me.
"Hugo must have really sold you on the idea
of the old boyfriend."

"Not at all," I said. "He just made me see
the story differently."

"What do you mean?"

The trail had segued from a quiet leafy
street as sedate and suburban-looking as
Homewood, up a gently sloping paved road
bordered by a lush golf course on one side

121

and the mountain on the other. Now we turned off the road and onto a generous path, which quickly became steeper as it wound toward the top of the mountain.

"You were right," I told Kelsey, beginning to huff a bit. "It doesn't need to be the story of my life. It can be any story I want it to be. The man can be any man I want him to be."

"So who do you want him to be?" Kelsey asked.

That was the challenge. Josh the character had been easy because he was based on Josh the man. Hugo the character — or rather, the character Hugo would play — could be anybody.

"We know he works at the publishing company," I said. "That part makes sense."

"It lets us tell work stories and personal stories at the same time," said Kelsey.

We rounded the first big curve, the one that showed us how far we had to go till the top.

"I'm not sure I love him being her boss," I admitted. "I mean, if I was supposed to be a twenty-six-year-old assistant, I wouldn't date the fifty-year-old owner of the company."

"Yeah, it's definitely kind of creepy in the age of Me Too," Kelsey agreed.

"So he can't be coming on to her while she's resisting," I said.

"And she can't be coming on to him, either," said Kelsey.

"They've got to do a lot of yearning," I said. "And brooding. If he's going to be her boss and you don't want it to get creepy, they can't do anything *besides* brood for a long time."

"Like Jane Eyre and Mr. Rochester," said Kelsey.

"Or Sam and Diane, or Jim and Pam," I pointed out, proud I'd been able to come up with TV references. "She definitely hates him."

"I thought she was supposed to love him!" Kelsey said.

"A long period of hate," I said. "And then at the end of the final season, one last intense act filled with love."

"Why does she hate him?"

"She sees him as . . . a playboy," I said. I was totally improvising. "He's a rich dilettante. Fifty-something years old, never married, has always dated younger women . . ."

"That sounds like Hugo Fielding," Kelsey said.

"Exactly."

We'd climbed high enough by that point to have a panoramic view of the downtown skyline. I still hadn't been to downtown LA, or anywhere else that looked like a city in the East Coast sense of the word. But from here, at least, we saw tall buildings close together, shining gold in the reflection of the setting sun. We gazed at the vista as we caught our breath, though I don't think either of us was seeing the view so much as the imaginary people in our heads.

"But he's not Hugo Fielding," Kelsey said. "He can be anyone we want him to be. Anyone who best serves Alice's story."

"I'm not sure how to decide that," I said.

"Let's start with figuring out his name," Kelsey said.

"James," I said.

That name felt right, always a good sign. It was like the spirit of the character announcing himself.

"You mean like . . . James Bond?" Kelsey said.

"Shit." Though I'd only come up with it a minute ago, I was already attached to the name James.

"I seem to remember Stella saying Hugo was trying to distance himself from that character," Kelsey said.

"Yeah, but fuck it," I said. "He gave me creative control over his character, so let's see if he really means it."

124

"All right," said Kelsey. "Maybe James is Mrs. Whitney's grandson."

I actually smacked her for that one.

"If Mrs. Whitney was his grandmother," I pointed out, "she'd be ninety years old and she'd be really pissed at you."

"Well, she can't be his mother, because then he seems like a mama's boy."

"What if she was his rich maiden aunt or something?" I said.

"Yeah," Kelsey said, growing excited. "Maybe she leaves him the publishing company after she . . ."

"Runs off to Costa Rica with a surfer dude."

"I love it." Kelsey laughed. "In the pilot, Alice could get hired by Mrs. Whitney, who immediately turns around and goes to Costa Rica, leaving the company in the hands of her hot nephew, James."

"James is a Brit," I said.

"He's not Hugo, remember," Kelsey said. "Or 007."

"Yeah, but if he's a Brit, he can have a life he left behind in London."

"Life meaning wife?" Kelsey said, raising her eyebrows.

"Not a wife," I said. I flashed on Zen. "Or a fiancée. Maybe an ex-wife."

"That's good," said Kelsey. "So he's *not*

125

the aging playboy Alice first takes him for."

"He's got kids," I said, imagining how nice it would be — for my character, I mean — to be with a man who wasn't looking to start a family. "But they're grown up and back in England with the ex."

"So he and Alice are actually kind of on the same level, although they're not aware of it," said Kelsey. "They're both divorced, they both have kids, they're both lonely . . ."

"They can't be too lonely." I laughed. "No one is going to believe that Stella Power and Hugo Fielding are spending years alone in New York not dating anyone."

"You're right," Kelsey said. "There are others. But no one is really right."

"Because Alice and James are perfect for each other," I said.

We were at the top of the trail now, where it broadened out and sloped gently to the lip of the canyon. People sat there playing with their dogs, watching the sun set. I heard the sound of a flute trilling up and down the scales, like a celebratory soundtrack to the vision Kelsey and I had created. And maybe to our friendship being back on track.

We started downhill, taking the narrow path. Theo was in the lead.

"I love the setup," said Kelsey. "But who

126

*is* James? How do you see him?"

"He's thoughtful," I said. "Kind."

"Sexy," said Kelsey.

"Do you think so?" I asked.

"Every woman in the world thinks so," said Kelsey.

"Would you date him?" I asked her. "I mean in real life."

"No, because he's an actor and we're working together, remember?" Kelsey said. "And even if those things weren't true, I doubt he'd be up for having a baby."

"I think that's true," I agreed.

"The question isn't would you date him, but who *would* you date?" Kelsey said. "That's who James should be."

"I don't want to date anybody."

"Yeah," Kelsey said. "But if you were a sane, untraumatized person who was ready to move on from her old life and start a new one, who would you fall in love with?"

"I'm not traumatized," I said, insulted.

"You spent the last two years living on a *rock*," said Kelsey.

"All right, so you're asking me to describe the man I would marry if someone held a gun to my head?" I said.

"I would not put it like that, but okay."

I had imagined such a man, hadn't I? I mean, when I'd imagined any man beyond

127

Josh. Someone like Paul Rudd only manlier, like Mark Ruffalo only taller, like Liam Neeson only younger, like James Gandolfini only more alive.

"Okay," I said. "He's close enough to my age that we like the same music, but bigger than me so we can't wear each other's clothes. Hairy, though not necessarily on his head. I'd rather be with a bald chubby guy than with somebody who wants to drag me out on a fucking run every morning."

"What if he likes to hike?" said Kelsey.

"Hiking is acceptable," I said. "I want somebody who's not going to get insulted if sometimes I sleep in the other room. Someone who knows what to buy me for my birthday. A good kisser. Independent. But warm. Can beat me at *Words with Friends* but is okay if I beat him." I thought a minute. "A good kisser. Did I already say that?"

It was turning seriously dark. If I had been by myself, I would have been scared. But Kelsey was confident on these trails, and I was confident that Theo would protect us, or at least that he would protect Kelsey, and maybe I could wedge my body in there so he'd have no choice but to protect me by association.

There was a howl, then another. At the

bottom of the hill, back on the road that ran along the golf course, there they were, a whole family of coyotes, arrayed on one of the greens. Kelsey quickly moved to clip Theo's leash to his collar, and just in time: The dog growled and strained against his leash toward the coyotes. The coyotes stood their ground and glared at us, eyes flashing as if they were the undead. They seemed to be reminding us that even though we were in one of the world's biggest cities, it contained many elements beyond our control, untamed.

Kelsey and I turned away and walked briskly, not talking, toward the well-populated street where we'd left the car.

When we were back in civilization and again breathing normally, Kelsey said, "Now that you've described your perfect man, you'll probably meet him in real life."

"I wasn't describing my perfect man so I could conjure him into being," I told her. "I thought we were creating a character."

"We are," said Kelsey. "But if you put that character out there, the universe will send him to you."

"That sounds like the kind of thing people believe in California," I teased.

"You'll see," said Kelsey. "The universe has been notified."

# Eleven

I was so excited that I was in LA for the opening of Maggie's art show at Hauser & Wirth, the most prestigious gallery in town. I wanted to support her debut in the West Coast art scene and I also wanted to show her a little bit of my new world. Given her children and marriage and white-hot career, I rarely got to spend five minutes alone with Maggie, never mind a whole evening.

I arrived at the gallery three hours before the party started, at the same time Maggie did, hoping to get a little time alone with her before everyone descended. But I was already too late. The gallery directors were there, of course, along with the art installers and the art critic for the *LA Times*. Then there was a photographer and a videographer, and then the caterers arrived.

So I wandered around, pretending to look at Maggie's egg sculptures, which I knew literally inside out. They were scattered across the cement floor of the huge industrial space, as if laid there by a chicken the size of Godzilla. Though I'd lived with the sculptures for years, they looked different in the California light, beaming down from the girded, skylit ceiling that was so high it might as well not have been there at all. They looked more alive, somehow, as if the intensity of the sunlight might prompt them to hatch.

There was something — or, you might say, someone — at the heart of each of Maggie's eggs, too. Inside was concealed another sculpture, a figure Maggie had carved and painted in the likeness of one of her creative heroines: Agnès Varda, Eva Hesse, Nina Simone. She'd photograph the figurative sculpture, to document its existence, and then encase it in plaster or clay or papier-mâché, layering and building the material until it assumed the shape of an egg.

The idea was that the emotional and artistic power embodied by the hidden sculptures would somehow emanate through the material that encased them. It was the three-dimensional answer, Maggie always told the artsy interviewers, to Sally Mann's photographs of the Civil War battlefields, ordinary meadows and woods whose vibration was somehow altered by the hor-

131

ror that had unfolded there. I interpreted this to mean that you could hide a truth inside a confection, and it would retain its power, something novelists did all the time.

It was after five when Maggie finally grabbed her garment bag and her makeup case and my hand, and pulled me into the bathroom, locking the door behind us.

"The *LA Times* guy told me the entire LA art world is turning out for this," Maggie said excitedly. "David Hockney, Catherine Opie, Barbara Kruger. Barbara Kruger, Liza!"

"I am so thrilled for you," I said.

I had been with Maggie every step of the way, from fourth grade art class where she was the only kid not making paper airplanes, through her cutting school in tenth grade to sit on the floor drawing at the Museum of Modern Art, through the scholarship to Cooper Union she won after her parents told her they would pay for her to study something practical like accounting, but not frivolous like art.

Maggie had lived without heat, she'd subsisted on rice and beans, she'd worked endless crap jobs, and she'd never compromised on her art. When I'd quit my publishing job to write full-time, Maggie was my role model. She showed me that you get up and start working every morning whether you feel like it or not, because you usually won't. That you had to be vulnerable enough to invest your tenderest emotions in your work, and tough enough to keep going when people rejected you.

Nobody wants you to be an artist or a writer, Maggie said. Not only did the world not care if you ever painted a picture or wrote a book, the world kind of wished you wouldn't. Your challenge was to do it anyway.

"How does it feel?" I asked her.

"Exciting," she said. "Unreal. The good thing about not being successful until you're fifty is that you know that, as wonderful as tonight is, the clock's going to strike midnight and what matters is what's waiting for you at home."

That was another thing Maggie had sacrificed to her art for years: a committed relationship. She had plenty of sex, but she always said she didn't have time to be in love. She had refused to even consider children. She'd always believed she could have a serious career or a family, but not both. After all, growing up in the New Jersey suburbs, we didn't see women who had both. And you know which one they had and which one they gave up.

"It's too bad Frankie couldn't be here," I said.

Although, much as I loved Frankie, I was glad they weren't here so I could have LA Maggie to myself. Well, to myself and the entire art world.

"You heard how Frankie feels about LA," Maggie said. "Plus we didn't want to drag the kids across the country or both be on this coast, leaving them on the other, especially with you out here too."

I didn't think she was trying to make me feel guilty, but I felt it anyway.

"I'll be your date tonight," I told her. "I'm excited about showing you LA. We're invited to a party later at Stella's."

It was Hugo who'd invited us, after I'd invited him to Maggie's opening. He said he'd love to meet Maggie, but he'd promised Stella he would help her set up her party, then urged me to bring Maggie to Malibu.

"I have to see what's happening here," Maggie said.

"Of course," I told her. "But Hugo will be there. He's looking forward to meeting you."

Maggie was by this point wearing a familiar-looking gold dress, the very one the stylist had tried to foist upon me the night of my book party. She was leaning over a sink, filling in her eyebrows.

"Remember when they used to call me CroMaggie in school because my brows were so thick?" Maggie said. "Now I have to paint on the individual hairs."

"Stella thinks I should have a face-lift."

"Don't you dare have a fucking face-lift," Maggie said.

"I won't," I assured her. "Maybe some filler . . ."

"Will you listen to yourself!" Maggie cried. "You've been kidnapped by the California pod people."

"When in Los Angeles," I said.

I reached into my purse and took out a tin of mints. I'd made my first trip to the weed dispensary that afternoon especially for this occasion. Maggie and I had smoked our way through high school and college, and then occasionally resumed the practice when we lived together during my second turn through my twenties.

But that was nothing like living in a city where there were billboards advertising weed delivery services and dispensaries that looked like Apple stores. Deciding between one artfully packaged edible and another was more like hand-selecting bonbons than silently exchanging cash for a baggy from some dude on a mountain bike. I thought Maggie would appreciate being able to partake without shivering on a street corner, hoping your kids (kids were the new parents) didn't catch you.

"I brought you a treat," I said to Maggie, holding out the tin.

"What's that?"

"Marijuana mints."

She looked at me as if I'd turned blue and started speaking in tongues.

"I'll pass," she said.

Ouch. She opened the bathroom door. The place was already pulsing. Before I stepped into the gallery, I slipped the mint under my tongue. I had the feeling I would have more fun if I was someone looser and more outgoing than myself.

Very quickly, the room was thrumming with people and noise and laughter. Maggie was swept away to meet this person and take a picture with that person, and I entertained myself with a glass of champagne and as many short rib mini tacos as I could inhale. Edible marijuana is the ultimate middle-aged high, requiring patience and delayed gratification. It would be at least another hour before I was high, and I was really wishing I'd taken that mint earlier.

This was a different crowd than I usually encountered in LA, not surprising given that I rarely ventured outside our writing cave at Kelsey's house or Stella's Malibu compound, a universe unto itself. The LA I'd come to know was a casual town — I was wearing a flowing satin blouse over ripped jeans and red suede booties, feeling like I was finally getting the LA dressing thing right — and this was a very un-casual event.

The gallery goers all seemed to be wearing eyeglasses that matched their outfits. Jewelry that they'd designed themselves. Their clothes telegraphed their wealth and rarified taste, but only to other rich people with equally rarefied taste. If you didn't know that shirt had cost $5,900 in Tokyo, you might think its wearer had made it himself using brown paper bags and mylar.

"Hey, baby," said a voice at my ear. It was Kelsey. "What's going on?"

Kelsey, at least, was dressed for the same party I was, though instead of a black satin shirt she was wearing an embroidered kimono over her torn jeans, and her booties were leopard print instead of red suede.

"I'm silently practicing my snarkiness," I told her. "Training for my return to New York."

"Angelenos practice plenty of silent snark," Kelsey said. "We just wrap it inside a smile, whereas you New Yorkers actually blurt it out."

"We're candid," I said.

"Harsh."

"Warm."

"Out of your fucking minds."

"Speaking of which," I said, "are you going to Stella's tonight?"

"No," Kelsey said. "Are you?"

"Maybe."

"I have a feeling it's going to be some kind of 'shroom fest," said Kelsey.

"Nobody told me that," I said.

Though that undeniably made the party more appealing to me rather than less, especially now that I was feeling the sparks from my magic mint starting to light up my brain.

"Whatever. I can't actually relax and have a good time around those people," she said. "It always feels like work."

"Maggie really wants to meet Hugo," I told Kelsey. "And I know she'd love seeing Stella's place."

"Be careful up there," said Kelsey. "Those things can get out of control."

"I don't even know if we'll go," I said. "I have to talk to Maggie."

"I'm going to find her and say hi, then I'm going home," said Kelsey. "Let me know what you end up doing later, okay?"

The rest of the event consisted of speeches, toasts, and standing alone pretending to be fascinated by the sculptures — which I was, especially since my mint had kicked in — while people crowded around Maggie, asking her to sign their catalogs.

And then they turned up the lights and the caterers started packing up everything, and it was just me and Maggie and the gallery directors and assorted famous artists and rich collectors, or at least people who were doing a good imitation of them.

"So, should we go to the party at Stella's?" I asked Maggie.

"Where is it?" she said.

"It's in Malibu."

"I have no idea what that means. Can we walk?"

What a New York question. Her acolytes were standing behind her, hungrily waiting to snatch her away. Or hey, maybe the weed was making me paranoid.

"We'd have to take an Uber," I said. "It'd take maybe an hour."

"An *hour*? What's there that's worth driving an hour for?"

139

"Hugo Fielding," I reminded her. "And according to Kelsey, there might be magic mushrooms."

I thought that might be an inducement. It was a night on mushroom tea in Jamaica that had first given Maggie the idea for her egg sculptures.

"I'm too old to do that kind of thing," Maggie said. "And so are you."

"It led to your biggest creative break-through!" I said. "Come on, this might be our last chance ever to do something like this."

Maggie opened her mouth, closed it again and shook her head in seeming exasperation, then opened it again.

"What's next?" she said. "Colonics? Scientology?"

"It's supposed to be like ten years of therapy in one night," I told her.

"That sounds like my version of hell," Maggie said. "When are you coming back to New York?"

"We have to finish writing the script and cast the other principal roles."

"This baby is not going to wait forever."

"A couple more weeks at the most."

She leveled a look at me that was at once disapproving and questioning. Part *Why are you doing this?* and part *WTF?* "Bottom-line truth, Liza: I'm worried about you. I've done this stuff. Don't take it lightly."

Her acolytes had begun to move away.

"We're going to Manuela's," the gallery director called.

"You're welcome to come with us," Maggie said to me.

"I thought we were going to spend tonight together," I said.

"Going to some celebrity party is not spending the evening together," said Maggie.

"Neither is going to an art world dinner."

I was hurt, but at the same time I got it. For her, this was work. She was being wined and dined by wealthy collectors and influential people in her field. Of course that's what she should do.

But I, I was high and primed to have some fun, yet sure I wasn't going to have any at the art dinner. I wanted to see Hugo. Possibly, I wanted to try those mushrooms.

The art world people were doing me a favor by making plain their disinterest. I didn't have to please anybody but myself now. I could do exactly what I wanted to do.

"This is my big night in LA," said Maggie. "Why can't you come support me? What's going on with you with the drugs and the guys and — what the fuck, Liza?"

I felt like a teenager. Partly because I was stoned, sure. And partly because Maggie sounded like my mother, telling me how bad I was to want to have fun with my friends instead of going to visit Grandma. Back then, when my mother yelled, I'd feel terrible and agree with her that I was a bad person and I'd do whatever she wanted.

But was that really true this time?

"You know, Maggie, I've been here for almost seven hours now. Most of that time I've been hanging around, supporting you, feeling proud of you, being happy just to be in your presence. I kept thinking we'd get some real time alone together, that we'd get to do something that was just about you and me."

"You knew I had all these work people to see."

"You're right, I did. I assumed I'd go along with you like I have lots of other times. But you know what, Maggie, I didn't have fun those times. You don't talk to me, you don't even really notice that I'm here. I'm not saying I want you to change. I'm saying I've changed. I love you, but I don't want to go to the damn dinner."

Maggie stood there, almost frozen, for a long minute. We stared at each other, gauging, I think, how solid we felt about each other, and about the collective us. All our other relationships, including with spouses and children and parents and siblings, had morphed over time and sometimes fell away. Our friendship was always at the center of everything, solid and stable as the earth beneath our feet.

But in California the earth could start shaking at any moment, I remembered, toppling bridges and cracking concrete and steel. Maggie and I gave each other a reassuring hug and kiss and moved in opposite directions, both turning at the same moment to wave. But I couldn't shake the unsettled feeling that the next time Maggie and I met, everything would have changed. Maybe it already had.

# TWELVE

When I arrived at Stella's, it was dark and fog was rolling in from the ocean. It always surprised me that no matter how hot it had been during the day, it was freezing at night in LA, as if the sun were the only source of warmth.

Shadowy figures moved around the lawn, illuminated with strings of Edison bulbs looped from one palm tree to the next. Dotted around the grass were Moroccan lanterns filled with candles. As I stood there alone, wondering how I'd neglected to bring a sweater, someone broke apart from the crowd and moved toward me.

"You're here," Hugo said. "I was worried you wouldn't make it."

"I'm here," I said, but I felt more nervous and uncertain about being there than I'd expected. I'd been so sure I wanted to come, and now I didn't know why. Maybe because it was stoned me who wanted to go to the party and straight me who was actually here.

Straight me also felt terrible about the skirmish with Maggie. I wished I were sitting in the restaurant at the edge of the booth, smiling and nodding and pretending I knew what the fuck anybody was talking about.

Hugo put his arm around me, but lightly, the way a brother might.

"You must be freezing," he said. "Let's get you one of these cashmeres."

He indicated three tall African baskets, one filled with black cashmere shawls, one with cream, and one with white.

"Where's Maggie?" Hugo asked, draping a white shawl over my shoulders.

"Out with her fans."

People were standing, chatting, all seemingly drinking the same clear liquid from heavy-looking crystal glasses. A young person as beautiful as a goddess appeared, a wine bottle in each hand, and asked whether I'd like oxygenated water or water collected from melted icebergs. She was dressed in a perfectly fitted white tee shirt and white jeans like a hot angel. At her elbow was another white-clad beauty, possibly male, bearing a silver tray holding crystal glasses.

"I'd go with the oxygenated," said Hugo.

145

"Very healing for the gum tissue," said the hot angel, smiling approvingly as I took a sip.

A third figure in white appeared bearing shot glasses full of smoothies containing, we were told, no salt, sugar, spices, gluten, legumes, or pork.

"What else is there?" I said, laughing.

While the server was pondering, Stella materialized, dressed in a long white satin gown that looked like something the Virgin Mary might wear to the Oscars.

"Welcome, traveler!" She leaned forward and kissed me on each cheek, and then did it again. "Are you ready for an amazing experience?"

In the distance the waves crashed and swished, in and out, in rhythm with the musicians playing near the pool: bongos, a ukulele, and a giant golden harp. It took me a minute to realize she was talking about the magic mushrooms.

"So the mushrooms are really happening?" I said, in a voice that sounded much more solid than I felt.

Stoned me had felt both relaxed and excited about trying new experiences. Straight me had kind of been hoping for white wine and a cheese plate and perhaps some discreet and strictly optional mushroom action down in the golf cart garage.

Stella clapped her hands three times and from somewhere a gong sounded. The white-outfitted wait staff stepped forward in unison, now bearing not bottles of iceberg water, but rough wooden crates of the kind expensive champagne comes in. A woman with long frizzy white hair, dressed in a white-and-silver kimono, appeared from the shadows behind Stella.

"That's Neoluna: New Moon," Hugo whispered. "She's the shaman."

Neoluna lifted her arms and tilted her face upward and implored the spirits to help guide our journeys, to show us everything that was good and protect us from evil.

I was from the generation that screamed and hid our eyes when the Wicked Witch came on the screen during the annual airing of *The Wizard of Oz.* Just hearing the word *evil* made me anxious.

Stella took one of the boxes from a waiter and held it out to Neoluna, who closed her eyes and hovered her cupped hands over the pale wood.

"What's she doing?" I whispered.

"Reiki," he whispered back.

One of the waiters in white appeared, proffering a wooden box in our direction. It was lined with a purple satin cloth and filled

147

with crystals, rough yet shimmery, a bed of them in sizes from baby carrot to jagged hot dog, white and pink and purple. And nestled in the crystals was a collection of long-stemmed, pale-colored desiccated mushrooms.

"What do you do with them?" I asked.

"You haven't done this before, have you?" asked Hugo.

"Not really."

He hesitated. "Are you sure you *want* to do it?"

*Was* I sure? Of course not. But soon enough I'd be back in New York, spending my days alone in a little apartment, typing from morning to night. If I felt really daring, I'd drink a Diet Coke after four p.m. Fuck yes, I was going to do this.

"Maybe take a half," Hugo said.

"We'll take two," I told the waiter, as if I were ordering from a pastry cart. I looked at Hugo. "In case."

Hugo and I found two vacant Moroccan poufs at the base of a palm tree, and he instructed me to eat half the mushroom, but some from both the cap and stem.

"How long will it take to kick in?"

"Maybe half an hour, forty-five minutes."

I took a bite. It tasted like thick expensive card stock, like a love letter that had been buried in a loamy forest and dug up by the light of a full moon.

"Why aren't you eating yours?" I asked him.

"I want to make sure you're okay."

I kept nibbling and masticating. I felt at once completely detached from Hugo, as if I were perched halfway up the palm tree gazing down at us, and at the same time as connected to him as if we'd been married for years.

"Maggie didn't want me to come here," I told him.

"Why not?"

"She was nervous for me?" That felt true but didn't feel like all of it. "And maybe hurt that I didn't stay with her." That still didn't feel like all of it. "And maybe scared that something bad would happen to me." Still not all. "And scared that if I had too much fun, I wouldn't go back to New York."

"Don't go back," he said, leaning closer.

My heart picked up speed and I felt a little woozy, but from the mushrooms or the closeness of Hugo, I wasn't sure. I examined what was left of my mushroom. I'd eaten the half that Hugo had prescribed.

"What happens if you don't take enough?" I asked him.

"You won't get high," said Hugo. "But

better that than too much. You'll know for next time."

There wasn't going to be a next time. I stuffed the rest of the mushroom in my mouth before Hugo could stop me. I chewed really quickly and swallowed hard.

He studied me for a long minute before he said, "That's okay. I'll be here."

"Maybe Maggie was right to be nervous," I said, pulling the white shawl closer around my arms. "It is scary being here all alone."

And I felt scared all at once, not in my mind but in my belly, as if I knew for sure that there was an actual murderer right there in the fog.

"You're not here all alone," Hugo said. "You're here with me."

He leaned yet closer, but as he did, I caught sight of a shadowy figure darting across the lawn, just beyond where the lanterns ended and the night began. I shivered, hard.

"I think I'm starting to feel something," I said.

I closed my eyes.

"Open your eyes if it gets too intense," Hugo counseled.

But it was too late for that.

If my life was a long smooth ride in a comfy car, the car had sailed through the bridge railings and crashed into the water. And now it was sinking through the black, black muck.

I flailed about trying to locate the image of someone I loved, someone alive who could pull me from this nightmare. Caitlin — baby Caitlin, little girl Caitlin, teenage Caitlin, grown-up Caitlin — flashed golden through my mind, like the sun appearing from between storm clouds. But then just as quickly the image of Caitlin fuzzed at the edges and grew transparent, as if she were a character I'd admired in a book or a movie I'd seen long ago. Someone who had never really existed.

"You have to tell me what's real," I said, groping in the darkness, not really sure who I was reaching for.

Hugo laughed. "Ah, what is reality anyway?" he said airily.

I grabbed the front of his shirt and shook. "Nooooooo!" I screamed.

"Okay," he said, patting me to calm me down. "You are real."

"Who am I?"

I felt incompletely tethered to the earth, as if I were floating above the ground, held down by a few fraying threads. I could descend into the muck or float up into the ether, those were my only options.

"You're Liza Miller," he said.

He had a reassuring grip on my arms now.

"Do I have any kids?" I asked him.

"You have a daughter, Caitlin, right?" he said.

"Caitlin is real?"

"Reportedly."

"What???" I snapped.

"Yes," he said, catching himself. "Yes, Caitlin is real."

"And the baby," I said. "Caitlin's baby. Is it real?"

"Yes," he said. "Yes, Caitlin is real. Her child is real. Kelsey is real. Stella is real. Maggie is real."

"Maggie is real?" That one sparked another wave of panic.

"Yes, Maggie is real and you are real and I am real."

"Who are you?"

"I'm Hugo Fielding, Liza," he said in a voice as careful and patient as a nursery school teacher's. "You know me."

"I don't know you," I said.

"Open your eyes, Liza. You can control this."

"You're lying to me," I said.

"I am not lying to you," he said.

He said it soberly, but there was a tone in his voice that sounded familiar. He didn't sound like Hugo, I realized. He sounded like James, the character I'd invented for him, telling Alice he wasn't interested in her. Lying.

"I am not lying to you," I repeated, mimicking his British accent. "You're such a fucking phony."

I could hear myself. I knew what I was saying. I knew how horrible it was and was horrified that I was saying it, but I meant it. I wanted to say it. Just maybe not out loud.

"I'm not a phony," Hugo said in his actor-y voice. I could almost hear the director whispering: *More sincere.*

"I'm not a phony," I said, in the exact same tone and rhythm. "Can't you fucking hear yourself?"

"I am not a phony," he said, in an exaggeratedly deep and steady voice that sounded like a guy in a pain reliever commercial. "What can I say to make you believe me?"

I burst out laughing. "*That* voice I believe," I said. "That voice I love."

Again, horrified. *Love?* Why did I have to use the word *love?*

"I love your voice, too," he said.

But he said it in that amused-sounding voice that sounded fake to my tripping self, and I told him so.

153

The next two hours passed pretty much like that, back and forth, me screaming and hallucinating and demanding and blurting outrageous things one minute, then asking Hugo if I could touch his ears the next. I mean, I kind of hated this version of myself, but it was a lot more fun being her than me.

It was like I had some special strain of Tourette's that made me say exactly the kind of things that would drive him away, even though my biggest fear was that he would leave. Like my husband had, like Josh had. But no, I reminded myself. I'd left them.

After what might have been twenty minutes or five hours, Hugo was able to persuade me to open my eyes. I was surprised to find the world still there, intact.

Hugo helped me to my feet and led me by the hand to two chaises by the edge of the pool. The musicians had disappeared, but there was music coming from speakers that must have been hidden in the eaves of the pool house: Sade or Erykah Badu, what Maggie always called *fuck music.* Each chaise held a thick, faux-fur afghan, the kind that only *felt* like the hair of dead animals, as if that were an ideal compromise. Under our individual pelts, we held hands and talked about our childhoods, his in small town Cornwall and mine outside New York.

The mushrooms had largely worn off, but had left me feeling like a gentler, more trusting version of myself. Our conversation wound its way around topics large and small, silly and sweet and dark. I told him about the Saturdays I'd spent with my dad in New York watching the Dancing Chicken and eating at Wo Hop, the trip to England where I met my husband, my brother's accidental death at eighteen — still, and I hope forever, the worst thing that had happened to me. He told me about his early days in London camping in a squat, his first trip to the U.S. on a freighter, even the much-ballyhooed story of his breakup with Stella.

"We were both really young, and she was sleeping with lots of other people too," he said. "But I fell in love with someone else. Which made me the bad guy."

"Someone else, meaning Madonna," I said.

"Right."

"So what was she like?"

"You're not really asking me that," he said.

"Why not?"

I thought it was a testament to how comfortable I'd grown with him that I *could*

155

ask him that, rather than pretending I had no interest in the topic.

"Because I'm not going to tell you anything really interesting," he said. "You or anybody else. She was intense, she was ambitious, she was magnetic. What was Josh like?"

"He was hot, he was beautiful, he was loving," I said. I hated to say those things out loud, not because they weren't true, but because they made me miss him. "And he was very young."

"So you two are not together anymore?"

"No," I said shortly. And then, because I wanted to change the subject as much as anything else, I said, "I'm sorry about tonight. I know I was horrible."

"It's okay. It's part of the experience."

"That was terrifying," I said. "You were heroic."

"How are you now?"

"Okay," I said.

I looked up at the sky. A vast network of stars shone through the scrim of fog, larger than normal stars and more brightly colored.

"It's like there are an infinite number of people and things and feelings out there," I said, "and I can reach up and pick whichever ones I want."

"Which do you want?"

He was looking at me as if he really expected an answer.

"I'll take a healthy family," I said blithely, pretending to pick it like a delicate flower from the sky. "Good friends. My writing. Inspiration. Trust."

"No man," he said. "Or woman, or . . . I mean, really, I'm judging from your book. I actually have no idea."

"Man," I said. "No."

"Why not?"

"Scared out of my fucking mind," I said.

"You said you didn't trust me."

"But now I do," I said.

He smiled. "You do?"

"Yes."

I let myself face him, let my eyes lock onto his. I felt like Ilse staring at Rick at the airport at the end of *Casablanca.* Kiss him, you fool.

I leaned forward. He pulled back.

"I would love to, believe me," he said. "When you're sober."

He permitted me to cuddle close to him, strictly for warmth. I dozed off with my head on his shoulder, and when I opened my eyes, the sky was starting to brighten.

I remembered everything, good and bad.

"I'm completely sober now," I said.

157

At this point I want it noted in the record that I could have fucked him right there on the chaise. And might have, if the patio lights had not blazed on.

"Here you two are!"

It was Stella, throwing open the glass doors at the back of the house, setting a thermos of coffee on the patio table. A few other revelers staggered out. Then some of the young people in white, seemingly as fresh in the gray dawn as they'd been last night, emerged bearing fruit and croissants and juice. I remembered what I'd screamed at Hugo at the beginning of the night: What's real? I still wasn't sure of the answer.

# THIRTEEN

I was jolted awake by a blast of bright sunlight when Kelsey pushed open the door of the guesthouse. I knew where I was: the white-painted beams of the ceiling, blackout shades, and cement floor of the guesthouse had come to feel like home to me. But Kelsey standing there was confusing. Though she was the owner of the guesthouse, and the main house where she lived was only thirty feet away, she had never come into this space before uninvited.

"You're alive," she said.

"What?"

"You never texted me last night to let me know what you were doing. I was so worried about you."

"I went to Stella's," I said, biting back the information that I was with Hugo, and that I'd been high out of my mind on mushrooms. "I fell asleep there. I didn't get home till it was light outside."

159

"You should have called me," Kelsey said. I struggled to sit up. "You're right," I said.

When I finally pulled my phone out of my bag in the car — a fleet of chauffeured Escalades waited outside Stella's to transport guests home — it was dead. Not that it had occurred to me at that point to call or text Kelsey.

"Maggie called this morning to check on you," Kelsey said. "So I guess you didn't go out with her after all."

"She went out with the art people."

"So was it a 'shroom fest?" Kelsey said. "As I predicted?"

I could have lied to her. But she would find out the truth soon enough.

"Yes," I said.

"And you took them?"

"I did."

"And?"

"It was horrible," I said.

"How was it horrible?" she asked.

"I thought I was under the ground with my dead ancestors."

"Jesus," she said. "I told you not to do that. That stuff can be really dangerous."

"It was all right," I said. "After the bad part, it turned really nice, and I got this incredible sense of trust and peace."

"Was somebody with you?"

160

I hesitated. "Hugo."

Kelsey groaned. "Liza, I don't know what's going on with you," she said. "You're acting more like a teenager now than you did when you were supposed to be in your twenties."

I sat up straighter. "It was one night, Kelsey. I wanted to try it. It's over."

"And you and Hugo?" she said. "Is that over too?"

"I don't know if there is a me and Hugo. But he really is a great person, Kelsey. I know you warned me about dating him, but I really like him."

"No!" Kelsey shouted. "I told you not to date an actor, and especially not to date an actor you're supposed to be working with."

I understood how that could be problematic.

"All right," I said.

"I am so furious at you," she said.

Maybe I had acted impulsively and irresponsibly. But I was an adult. No one had been hurt.

"Okay," I said. "But I don't get why you're so upset about this."

She thought for a long minute. "I'm afraid you're going to screw up the show," she admitted.

161

"I'm not going to screw up the show," I said.

"You're fighting with one star and you're taking drugs with the other one. That's not acceptable."

She was right. "I don't want to screw up the show, Kelsey. I'm sorry."

"You're going back to New York and publishing and writing when this is over," she said. "This is my business. Whatever happens with this is going to stick to me forever."

I felt stricken. "I'm sorry. I really am. Tell me what you want me to do. If you want me to go back to New York, I'll go."

"You tell me what *you* want to do. Decide, Liza," she said. "If you want to stay here, I'll be thrilled, but you have to pull it together and act like a professional."

"I hear you," I said.

"That means no starting fights about the plot, and going along with any changes they want to make."

I hesitated. "I thought everyone had signed off on the outline."

Kelsey and I, along with Hugo and Stella, had turned it in to the network last week.

"They have," she said.

"So I thought that meant they weren't going to ask for any more big changes."

162

"Everybody said they loved it," she told me.

"Okay, so now we just write to the outline they saw and look for the principal actors, and then we're done in LA, right?" I said.

"That's right," she said.

"Sounds like a week, maybe two?" I said. She said that should do it.

I said that sounded fine.

We agreed that I would write the first draft of the script, while she would work on casting. I think we were both looking for a way to keep working together without actually working together.

I said I'd stay, she said she was glad, we gave each other a little hug. Then we retreated to our separate corners.

The experience with the mushrooms and its aftermath made me ready to leave LA in the way that Maggie's lectures and Caitlin's pregnancy could not. It wasn't the scariness of the mushroom trip that made me want to go back; that had actually left me with a new appreciation for the beauty of everyday life. And it had given me a sense of trust in Hugo that I don't think I'd ever felt with another man. He'd seen my worst and he hadn't flinched.

It was more that I'd ventured to the end

of the plank in terms of LA experiences —
gone as far as I was willing to go at the
literal edge of the country — and the only
thing to do now was turn back. There were
many things that were wonderful about Los
Angeles: the beaches, the canyons, the food,
the houses, the weather so perfect it didn't
seem real. But I couldn't imagine it ever
feeling like home, and after yet another stop
along the road, I wanted a home more than
ever.

I felt as if I'd ventured to the end of the
plank with Hugo, too. I'd gone as far as it
made any sense to go, and remaining in that
Cathy-and-Heathcliff state of perennial
wanting and not having was torture. Hugo
and I exchanged some texts after the night
of the mushrooms, but after reassuring him
that I was fine, I told him I was working too
hard on the script to get together.

This was in fact true. I'd wake up at about
seven, brew some coffee while I answered
the morning's emails from the East Coast,
and then start writing. It was fun and easy
writing the screenplay — a lot easier than
writing a novel — now that Kelsey and I
had broken every beat in the scene and the
episode. All that white space! No phony
descriptions or boring interior monologues!

Sometimes it would be seven p.m. and I'd

still be lying on my bed or in the hammock in my nightgown and one of Kelsey's cashmere sweaters, typing madly, having walked a grand total of thirty-eight steps that day.

Kelsey spent that time working with the venerable casting director Carlotta Dunn, lured out of forced retirement after #MeToo, looking at actors for the remaining major parts: Maggie; the daughter character; and Kelsey's own character, Lindsay.

Once a draft of the script was finished, Carlotta arranged a "chemistry read" at Whipple Studios with Stella and Hugo and the other prospective leads. We were already settled into the audition room when Hugo and Stella arrived. This was the first time Hugo and I had seen each other since that night. He sat down across from me, laying a dog-eared copy of *Younger* on the table, and flashed me a quick smile. I smiled back but kept my eyes trained on the script, hyperaware of Kelsey at the table watching my every move.

Carlotta handed around headshots and résumés for each of the actors. First up was a young woman who was reading for the part of Alice's daughter, Diana, aka Caitlin. Marissa was from Atlanta, where she'd been acting in local theater and commercials since she was a child. She had been in LA for a year and had already been cast in several speaking roles on TV shows and in movies.

Marissa was small, blond, and very pretty. She was nineteen but could easily have passed for fourteen or twenty-four. She looked like she might have been the love child of long, lanky Stella and a jockey.

She and Stella were reading one of the first scenes in the script, where Alice, fresh from a discouraging round of ageist job interviews, calls Diana where she's studying in India and breaks the news that she's selling the family home. That wasn't the way it happened in real life or in the book — it was a more gradual process than that — but we'd fast-forwarded this part for the pilot:

**DIANA**
Mom, this is the third time you've called me this week.

**ALICE**
I wanted to let you know that I'm putting the house on the market.

**DIANA**
Mom, you can't do that while I'm halfway

across the world. I need time to say good-bye.

Stella/Alice's next line was supposed to be "Then come home and help me pack," but Stella said, "Then come hope and welp me . . . oh, golly, I'm sorry."

Four times we listened to Marissa say, "I need time to say goodbye," and four times Stella flubbed her response. Finally, she broke down laughing, shaking her head and getting to her feet. Holding out her arms to Marissa, Stella said, "Come over here and help me forgive myself for being such a ginormous idiot."

"We'll be in touch," Carlotta told Marissa. Once Marissa had left the room, Carlotta picked up the next headshot in her stack. "The next Diana trained at your alma mater, Hugo, so she'll probably be easier to work with. . . ."

"Let's come back to this character later," said Stella.

We moved on to the Lindsays.

Lindsay was Kelsey's character. Before the first actress came into the room, Kelsey leaned across the glass table and said, "I just want to establish that I went for actresses who looked as unlike me as possible."

The idea was to find an actress to play Lindsay who would be a physical counterpoint to Stella's Alice, who was tall, thin, blond, and gorgeous.

The first actress, Jenny Chin, was about the same height and weight as Stella, but Asian. Jenny looked nothing like the real life "Lindsay," who was of course sitting at the table with us, but she and Stella looked great together. And I loved the way Jenny delivered her lines: confident, ambitious, Kelsey's thespian soul sister.

They were playing the scene where Lindsay and Alice meet for the first time in the ladies' room at the fictional Gentility Publishing, after Alice lands her job, which indeed was how and where Kelsey and I first met:

**ALICE**
*(fist pumps at the mirror)*
Yes!

LINDSAY, the perfect young professional, enters the ladies' room.

**LINDSAY**
*(catching Alice's eye in the mirror)*
What's so thrilling?

168

**ALICE**

I just got a job. I'm going to be an assistant to James Churchill, head of marketing.

**LINDSAY**

Congratulations. Or maybe I should say, my condolences.

Jenny delivered her lines with energy and emotion. Stella, on the other hand, sounded as if she were reporting that her dog had died.

We tried a couple of different scenes before thanking Jenny for her time.

"I thought she was terrific," Hugo said.

"Terrific," Stella agreed. "Is there anyone else?"

The next prospective Lindsay was a gorgeous biracial actress named Dara Fuchs, who had deep dimples and was a bit shorter and a lot curvier than Stella. She delivered Lindsay's lines in a more sardonic, subdued way than Jenny had, but this time Stella's acting was so over the top, I wondered whether she'd dropped a tab of speed.

"She was awesome too," Hugo said when Dara left the room.

"Awesome," Stella agreed.

"Why don't I try reading with both of them?" Hugo said.

"Maybe we could see the next person," said Stella.

"Is something wrong?" Hugo asked.

The rest of us held our breath.

"Is something wrong with you?" Stella said.

With a sigh, Hugo leaned back and swiveled in his chair.

"Do we have anyone for Maggie?" Hugo asked.

"I have a verbal commitment from someone I'm really excited about," Kelsey said. "Debi Mazar."

I had heard this news and was equally thrilled. "I loved her in *Entourage,*" I said. I used to watch that with Caitlin when she was in high school.

"Debi's fabulous," said Hugo. "But I didn't know she was open to doing another series."

"She is since we're shooting in New York," Kelsey said.

Stella stood up. "Excuse me," she said.

While she was out of the room, we talked about when production might start on the pilot, what we'd thought of the two Lindsays, and whether we'd seen any other actresses who might work for the daughter role.

We needed Stella's input on all these questions, but time passed and she did not return. Finally, Kelsey texted her. Then called her.

"She's not picking up," Kelsey said.

"Should we make sure she's okay?" I asked, imagining that we'd check the bathroom first, in case she'd gotten sick, and then the patio, where she might be vaping or tripping her brains out. And then we'd call the police.

I saw a glance flick between Kelsey and Carlotta. Carlotta stood up.

"I'm going to have to talk to Fernando," she said.

"Hold off for a bit," snapped Kelsey.

"Let me try to reach Stella," Hugo said.

He typed quickly with his thumbs. A few seconds later, his phone chimed with a response. He held it at arm's length and squinted.

"Ttyl," he read. "What's that mean?"

"Talk to you later," said Kelsey.

He typed again, something quick, and then his message whooshed out into the universe.

"What did you say?" I asked him.

"WTF," he said, looking around at us. "I know that one."

"We're all very excited about *Younger*," Fernando Vasquez said, his face smooth and immobile. He might have been twenty-four or, I don't know, eighty-four. I couldn't tell anymore, and I didn't care. Fernando was Barry Whipple's number two: On any major money or creative decisions, Fernando needed to be consulted. In fact, if I hadn't actually seen Barry, I might have assumed Fernando *was* Barry.

Fernando had called personally and asked Kelsey and me to come in for a meeting the morning after Stella's disappearance. He assured us that Whipple had no intention of cancelling the show, that in fact they had huge plans for it. They just had a few small adjustments they wanted us to make before we started shooting.

"We adore the Liza character," Fernando was saying now.

"Alice," I said.

"What?"

"The character's name is Alice. I'm Liza."

"Oh, right," said Fernando. "We'll have to look at the market research on the name. We're thinking maybe Liza's origin story isn't boring New Jersey housewife but some kind of executive."

"I wouldn't call Alice *boring,*" I said. "And the whole reason she pretends to be younger is to get a job after spending years at home

172

with her daughter."

"Of course, of course," Fernando said. "We love that. I mean, ageism, grrr, right? But we were thinking, what if she was an executive, like maybe head of the publishing company, but then she decides she wants to be an actress?"

"Interesting," said Kelsey.

Okay. Though the word I might have used was *absurd*.

"And so she starts going to auditions," Fernando said, growing more excited, "and people want to cast her because they're like, *Oh my God! You're so young and beautiful!* But then they see her résumé and they go, *Ew, dude, she is crusty!*" Fernando slapped his black leather desk chair as if he were trying to spur it into a gallop.

"That kind of thing certainly happens a lot in the business," Kelsey said. I did admire her diplomacy.

"Right?" said Fernando. "And wouldn't it make more sense for her to be discriminated against in an industry that was all about youth and beauty?"

"But in a way, how old you look can be a bona fide qualification for an acting job," I said, trying to mimic Kelsey's even tone. "Ageism is more outrageous when your job performance has nothing to do with age or looks."

"We're concerned that the stakes could be higher," Fernando said. "She wouldn't have to be an actress. She could be a model. Or a rock star."

I burst out laughing, then clapped my hand over my mouth. "That is a *hilarious* idea," Kelsey said, as if she were clarifying.

"And about the fortysomething," Fernando continued, "we were thinking that maybe she's in her thirties."

"Thirty-eight or thirty-nine?" I said.

"Or thirty-three."

"The story doesn't work unless the heroine is being discriminated against because of her age," I pointed out. "There isn't much ageism against thirty-three-year-olds."

"There is if they want to be rock stars!" Fernando exclaimed. "Or models."

"Or actresses," Kelsey said. "Or even showrunners, haha."

Was she actually agreeing with him?

"Liza's daughter is supposed to be in college," I said.

"We're thinking maybe the daughter is younger," Fernando said.

"You mean, high school younger?" I said.

Certainly plausible, and a teenager would be old enough to be at home alone while her mom worked, but was Liza going to be honest with her daughter about her age charade, or was she going to change clothes on the train to and from the city every day? I was trying to be accommodating, but I was having trouble envisioning how the whole thing would work.

"Or grade school," said Fernando. "Or kindergarten. Or even younger, haha."

"Maybe Alice only *wants* to have a baby," said Kelsey.

"Interesting!" said Fernando. "Maybe she's knocked up and she doesn't know whether Josh or James is the baby daddy!"

"There's no more Josh," I said.

"Whaaaaaaat?" said Fernando. "I *love* Josh."

"Stella made us get rid of him and create James so Hugo could be in it," I said. "You signed off on that."

"Which was a *brilliant* idea," said Kelsey.

"So if you're going to want a big baby daddy drama, it's going to have to be between James and some guy she meets in an alley," I said.

"Ooooooh, edgy," said Fernando.

"I wasn't serious!" I cried. "It's a terrible idea to make her want a baby! This whole thing is about a woman trying to reclaim her independent life after she's raised her child. *That's* the drama. It's not: *Which highly insane coupling produced this completely ill-advised pregnancy?* It's not: *Will Liza be able to balance work and family?* She will not! She will quit her job and stay home with her kid, and twenty fucking years later, she'll try to get back into the work world and find out the world doesn't want her!"

I was panting. Possibly sweating.

"Alice," Kelsey said.

"What?"

"You said, *Will Liza be able to balance work and family?* I think you meant Alice, the character. Will *Alice* be able to balance work and family," Kelsey said.

"Alice, that's right. Alice the character," I said, "who was a forty-four-year-old mom of a college-age daughter living in New Jersey and trying to get back into the publishing business in New York. Just like me."

"We have a New York set that looks *totally* like the real thing," Fernando said. "Unless we decide to go with the actress or rock star idea and move the setting to LA."

"Are you saying you're shooting this in LA?" I asked.

"I swear, you'll never know the difference," said Fernando.

"We can make that work," said Kelsey. But

she wasn't looking at me. Because she knew that was where I drew the line.

There was a real difference, after all, between me and Alice in the book. Alice was fictional and I was real. They could do whatever they wanted with Alice and it didn't change anything for me or affect my life at all. It didn't have to, I meant. I didn't have to let it.

Maybe that was why I kept clinging to the fiction that the book *was* fiction: Because if I turned those years of pretending to be younger into a story, I could cut them loose from my life. *Go be a TV show,* I could tell that whole lying, faking part of me. And I, the me who looked and acted like the same person I really was, would be free to live my real life in the here and now.

The real me, the almost-fifty-year-old me, knew it was time to let my book go, just as it was time to let that part of my life go. Staying here, continuing to battle, was not good for the show, was not good for Kelsey, and was not good for me. I knew what I had to do, and I knew how to do it because I had quite recently seen it done by a master.

"Excuse me," I said. Then I left the room.

# FOURTEEN

From the Uber, I texted Kelsey. I apologized for slipping away and said I didn't want to continue arguing, but I also didn't want to work on the show as it had developed. I thanked her for giving me a chance to be involved, said I was looking forward to seeing the finished product, and that I'd get in touch with her when I was back in New York.

Kelsey immediately began texting me back. First she was confused. Then she was demanding. And in the end she was angry, which might have been what she'd been feeling all along. I ignored her as best I could. I made my plane reservation for a flight four hours from now, but given LA traffic, I was not going to get to the airport that early. My Uber had not even made it to the 405 when Hugo called.

"Don't go," he said.

"How do you know I'm going?"

"Stella called," he said.

"How does Stella know?"

But as soon as I said it, I realized that while I'd been thinking I'd learned how things *really* worked in Hollywood, I'd missed what was most obvious.

"Stella was behind all this, wasn't she?" I said.

"I'll talk to her," he said. "She likes to play games. Really, you can't go. I don't want to do the show without you."

"Okay," I said.

"Okay? You'll stay?"

"No," I said. "Okay, don't do the show."

"How can you let it go like that? This is your baby."

"It isn't my baby anymore. It's Kelsey's baby. And Stella's and Fernando's and yours, I guess. The baby I care about now is the real one my daughter is having in a few months in New York."

He was quiet for a moment.

"All right," he said finally, quietly. "I understand. But please come over to say goodbye? For a few minutes. Then I'll take you to the airport."

I hesitated. "You can't try to talk me out of going or tell Kelsey I'm there or make me feel guilty."

"I just want to kiss you goodbye," he said.

179

Hugo's house was surrounded by an eight-foot-high wall covered with lush vines. At the entry was a tall and shiny red door studded with heavy black nails. Had this been a fairy tale, I would have been on the lookout for poison apples or wicked stepmothers. Above the door was a large brass bell from which dangled a long knotted black cord. I yanked and practically blew out my eardrum.

"Sorry, sorry!" came Hugo's voice from behind the door.

And then his beaming face appeared. He looked like he'd just gotten out of bed, his hair sticking up every which way, his beard thick but not furry. He was wearing bagged-out gray sweatpants and a frayed gray tee shirt that read *After Cacciato.*

"I took a writing class with Tim O'Brien," I said, pointing to his shirt. O'Brien wrote the Vietnam novel *Going After Cacciato.*

"That was the name of my older brother's band," said Hugo.

He reached out and pulled me inside the red door. It was like stepping into an enchanted land. The yard looked like Eden after the gardener had come through, with

180

bright green neatly trimmed grass and manicured rosebushes. It was lush with trees dangling lemons from every branch and hydrangeas as big as your head and butterflies flitting over babbling fountains. His house looked like the kind of cottage where a hunky woodsman might live, all rough brown clapboards and leaded-glass windows and dark green shutters with clovers cut into them. The wicked stepmother vanished and in her place arrived whistling elves and dancing princesses.

"I can't believe this place," I said.

"I bought it when I first came to LA and thought I'd only be staying for a few months here and there, and now I hate to leave."

"I don't blame you," I said. I felt so much more envious of this place than I did of Kelsey's or even Stella's. As a native New Yorker, it was crazy to be in a city that was filled with charming cottages and light-filled midcentury houses and grand old apartment buildings that looked like palaces. You could live in the heart of Los Angeles and still be surrounded by quiet and green. Though as I now knew, there were snakes in that grass.

My phone buzzed again. I looked at it. Sure enough, another text from Kelsey.

"I'm shutting this thing down," I said,

deliberately powering it off and burying it in my bag. "I have an hour."

Hugo didn't respond. Instead, he gathered me into his arms and kissed me, a kiss that was soft and insistent, passionate and eternal. I hadn't been kissed in two years. I hadn't been kissed this well in . . . maybe since Josh and I got back together that last time. Or maybe ever? Right now it felt like ever.

Had kissing always been this good? Because if so, why didn't everybody do it all the time?

We kept kissing. There was the kiss and how amazing that felt, infinitely soft and hard at the same time. And then there was the knowledge that the person on the other end of those lips was Hugo Fielding. That the quite substantial penis that was pressing into my hip was attached to his hips.

A phone began dinging with an incoming text.

"I thought I turned that off," I mumbled. We kissed. *Ding. Ding ding ding!*

"Oh, shit," he said. "That's mine."

"It's probably Kelsey."

"Sorry."

He fished it from his voluminous sweatpants, examined the first one for a moment, then handed it to me.

182

The texts were indeed from Kelsey.

*Is Liza with you? Her friend Maggie is trying to reach her,* the first one read.

And then, *If you hear from her, her daughter's in labor.*

I experienced a deep sense of dislocation of the kind you get in a hot place in the middle of winter. Didn't Caitlin have at least eight more weeks to go? Had I completely — even kind of psychotically — lost track of time?

I powered my phone back on to see the flood of texts and calls from Maggie. I tried calling first. She didn't pick up but texted immediately.

*At the hospital,* Maggie wrote. *C's water broke. Come asap.*

*Omw,* I typed.

I had forgotten Hugo was even standing there.

"I've got to go," I said.

"What's happening?"

"My daughter's having her baby."

More than eight weeks early. How big would the baby be? Could it even survive? I couldn't help thinking about that and at the same time tried to shut that possibility out of my mind.

"I'll get a plane for you," he said.

183

"I'm already on the first available flight," I said.

I was calculating in my head: Half an hour to LAX, then through security, then a five-hour flight, minimum. Another half hour to make my way out of JFK, plus another hour to get to the hospital in Manhattan. In fucking rush hour! So maybe two hours. In all, that was — fuck! — nearly ten hours to get to my daughter's side.

"No," Hugo said. He was already on his phone. "I mean a private plane."

Whoa. The airport was right in Santa Monica, Hugo said. It didn't make sense to get a helicopter. He'd take me on the Ducati.

Which was apparently a motorcycle.

I'd never really inhabited the world of people who do whatever they want whenever they wanted, and I wish I'd been able to enjoy it, but speeding down the Pacific Coast Highway, clinging to Hugo's back, all I could think about was Caitlin. And the baby. My grandchild. But mostly Caitlin, my baby.

*What the fuck was I doing here? Why wasn't I with her where I belonged? I'd chased a rabbit through the looking glass, but what was I searching for? What was there on earth that was more important than her?*

184

When we reached the little airport in Santa Monica, Hugo roared through the parking lot and right out onto the tarmac. Everyone seemed to know him there. The plane was waiting. It was dramatic and even romantic, but at the time, it all — I mean the movie star and the motorcycle and the waiting plane — seemed like natural elements to bridging the time and space that separated me from my child.

He walked me up the stairs onto the plane, which was outfitted with an all-cream leather interior. He gave me a warm, reassuring hug, and in that moment I felt toward him like I might toward an older brother, maybe the person my own brother might have been had he not been killed by that hit-and-run driver.

I pulled back from Hugo and simultaneously pushed him away.

"Thank you so much," I said.

Meaning: Now please get off the fucking plane and let me go.

He kissed his fingertips and then touched them to my cheek. And then he was gone, and, ten minutes later, I was miles and miles away, above the earth, speeding through the clouds to New York.

# FIFTEEN

Less than five hours later, the jet landed at
Teterboro Airport in New Jersey. The only
thing I'd noticed throughout my flight was
my phone. There was an empathetic flight
attendant named Andy who did his best to
tempt me with drinks and food, but all I
wanted was water and tea. Finally, he
brought me an enormous comforter, a down
pillow, and a Xanax and told me to press
the button if I needed anything else, but
otherwise he'd leave me be.

Maggie kept sending reassuring texts, saying everything was fine, labor was progress-
ing slowly, I would make it in plenty of time.

Hugo had arranged a helicopter to meet
me at the airport in New Jersey. I had never
been in a helicopter before, but I experienced it only as a magical way to transcend
the traffic that clogged every artery that
crossed the river between New Jersey and
New York City. We traveled to the roof of

Caitlin's hospital in less time than it would have taken us to drive across the George Washington Bridge.

Maggie was waiting on the helipad with a member of the hospital staff, and escorted me downstairs, her arm locked firmly in mine.

"Is everything still all right?" I asked her breathlessly.

"Yes, it is," she said firmly.

"I can't believe I made it in time. Where is she?"

"I'm bringing you to her now," she said.

She gripped my bicep and steered me down hallways that felt dark and silent. I expected every door we approached to be Caitlin's. We passed the nursery, where babies that looked too big to be newborns slept and squalled, before Maggie guided me through a door she opened with a special pass she wore around her neck, like someone who worked here.

"Is this the way to the labor room?" I asked hopefully, excited to have nearly reached the end of my journey. Any second I'd be holding my daughter's hand, watching my grandchild take her first breath, resuming my place as a guardian angel making sure everything went all right.

Maggie didn't answer. We turned another

corner and came to stop in front of a glass wall, behind which there were medical personnel in full protective gear standing around futuristic equipment.

"What's this?" I asked, suddenly afraid of new things.

"This is your granddaughter," Maggie said. There was a slight smile on her face as she inclined her chin toward one of the pieces of equipment. It was a transparent box, I saw now, elevated on a steel platform with vents and tubes running from it to various other pieces of equipment. And inside the clear box, I could just make out a tiny scrap of a human.

"You mean . . ."

"Three pounds, twelve ounces," Maggie said. "She's a fighter."

"Oh my God, I can't believe it happened already."

"It happened right after your plane took off. They did an emergency C-section."

"You should have told me," I said to Maggie.

If there had ever been another time Maggie had withheld information so central from me, I wasn't aware of it.

"I knew how terrible you'd feel missing her birth, and how worried you'd be," Maggie said, "and there was nothing you could do anyway."

I understood why she felt that way, maybe even appreciated that she'd tried to protect me from anxiety and heartache and guilt that I wouldn't be able to channel into any productive action. But at the same time, deliberate dishonesty from someone I had always relied on to tell me the truth made me deeply uneasy.

I focused on my tiny granddaughter. All the feelings Maggie had tried to shield me from washed over me. It seemed miraculous that she could survive at all, no matter how many tubes they connected to her. The doctors and nurses all seemed busy and distracted; no one was gazing at her as if they could keep her alive by their attention alone. I wanted to do that. But I wasn't allowed to get that close, and as hard as I might have wished my presence would make everything all right — wasn't a mother supposed to have that power? — I knew that in fact I was as helpless as I'd been when I was trapped in the airplane.

When I'd imagined this moment, I'd seen myself searching the baby's face and body for evidence of a resemblance to Caitlin, or to me, or to my parents and brother, all now gone so long ago. I'd hoped Caitlin would have red hair like my brother, the red hair I had always envied, and since his death longed to see reborn. But Caitlin was blond like her dad had been when he was younger, and it was too soon to tell with this start of a child. She looked unfinished, not ready for the world.

Then a tall figure dressed in a hospital gown, a green cotton cap over his hair and a mask over his face, moved over to my granddaughter's incubator. A nurse helped him slip his hands into the glove-like portals that extended inside the plastic. His hands looked almost as big as the entire baby. I assumed the man was a doctor, until I realized, thanks to his height, that it was Ravi. That was reassuring for two seconds, until I wondered why he was there alone.

"Where's Caitlin?" I said.

"They wanted her to try and sleep," said Maggie.

"I want to see her," I said.

Maggie hesitated for long enough that I thought she might refuse to take me to my daughter, in which case I would find my way by myself. But instead Maggie nodded and led me back into the maze of corridors, taking me up the stairs when the elevator proved too slow. Finally, we were in the maternity ward. Walking down the hallway past half-open doors, I was able to glimpse

190

new mothers, sometimes with their partners or families, sometimes alone, sometimes with their baby in their arms or asleep in a plastic bassinet beside the bed. I remembered how utterly delicious and fantastic those first hours were, lying in my bed after the storm of labor, staring at this human being I had created. It was the closest, mushroom trip included, that I'd ever come to seeing God.

And my daughter wasn't going to have that. Because her daughter was shut away in a special facility on another floor. So Caitlin couldn't hold her — oh God, I'd completely forgotten to ask the baby's name! — and the baby could not be held. What a loss for both of them.

We turned a corner and walked through a door and there was my baby, still awake but looking wan and very lonely.

I burst into tears, *Caitlin* burst into tears, and all up and down the hospital corridors, babies started crying. Caitlin and I both stopped our wailing, horrified by what we'd set off, then looked at each other and burst out laughing. Which made us hug and both start crying again.

"I wanted you," Caitlin said into my ear.

I couldn't tell whether Maggie had heard,

but I didn't really care.

"I'm so sorry I wasn't here," I said. "That must have been really frightening."

It felt so good to hold my little girl in my arms, though it seemed cruel that I got to do that when Caitlin didn't.

"It's okay. Ravi and I took care of everything," Maggie said.

As grateful as I felt toward Maggie, I wanted to slug her. I didn't need her to tell me it was okay I wasn't there; it wasn't okay, and it never would be. She and Ravi may have taken care of a lot of things in my absence, but they couldn't take care of me being there when my daughter needed me.

"I'm here now," I told Caitlin, smoothing her hair.

"Did you see her?" Caitlin said. And then, sounding more panicky, "Is she okay? I should be with her."

"She's beautiful," I said.

"I have to go see her," Caitlin said, trying to pull away from me and climb off the bed. "I have to make sure she's still breathing."

I held on to Caitlin.

"Ravi's with her," said Maggie.

"Would you go check on them?" I asked Maggie.

For a moment, I thought that Maggie was going to refuse — we had just been down there, after all, and there was nothing she could really do or see from the corridor — but then she seemed to understand that Caitlin needed the reassurance, and I needed a little time alone with Caitlin.

"I'll let you know how everything is going," Maggie said, slipping back out of the room.

Then it was just me and Caitlin.

"I shouldn't have been working so much," Caitlin said. "I was running around, trying to make everything perfect. I'm a *terrible* mother. . . ."

"Shhhhhhhhhh," I said. "This didn't happen because of anything you did. You're going to be a wonderful mother."

Caitlin's eyes grew wide and scared. "What if she dies?" she whispered.

"She's not going to die. We will all make sure of that. You need to sleep now. You'll see her in the morning, and everything will be all right."

I cranked down her bed, fluffed her pillows, dimmed the lights, pulled her covers up over her shoulders. Then I took her hand and sat there waiting for her breathing to grow calm and regular, feeling my own eyes become heavy, just like when she was a toddler and I sat with her to help her fall asleep. I could not believe that this morning I'd been in a meeting with Fernando, then in Hugo's arms, and now here. Today Caitlin became a mother, my granddaughter became a person, and the world became a place brimming with new dangers and new love.

# SIXTEEN

Three days later, they sent Caitlin home from the hospital without her baby. She'd had a C-section, which is major abdominal surgery, so she was in pain and her hormones were going crazy, but she couldn't rest because she hated to leave the baby — Eloise, after Caitlin's favorite childhood heroine — alone.

Ravi had been able to take emergency medical leave around the baby's birth, but he got only two weeks of paid parental leave and he wanted to save that for moving, bringing Eloise home from the hospital, and any emergency that might arise in the meantime. Ravi invited me to move into their tiny apartment and sleep on the fold-out love seat, so I could be there with Caitlin when he had to work long shifts. He also wanted me to help Caitlin get back and forth to the hospital and manage the doctors and treatments. Ultimately, of course, he and Caitlin both knew far more about the worlds of hospitals and medicine than I did, and were perfectly capable of handling Eloise's care by themselves. But it was clear my presence was considered some kind of talisman against the frightening and unexpected. I was supposed to keep away the bogeyman. We all almost believed I could.

Poor Caitlin was pumping milk when she wasn't crouched by Eloise's incubator, stroking her back and telling her how much she loved her. They wouldn't let me in the NICU yet, so I stood on the other side of the glass, watching in awe. My baby's baby. The mother's mother. There's nothing like having your first grandchild to bring alive the feeling that you're one link in a chain that stretches back through the ages and will go on, God willing, into the future long after you're gone. It's amazing how the same thing can make you feel completely insignificant and cosmically important at the same time.

The fact that she was a self-aware, educated mother, a member of the health profession who'd been conscientious throughout her pregnancy, seemed to make Eloise's premature birth and extended hospital stay more rather than less difficult for Caitlin. Modern pregnancy and baby guides make parents feel that all they have to do is follow the rules and their children will be healthy, their pregnancies and births will go smoothly, and they'll never have to deal with the kinds of complications and risks that befall expectant mothers who smoke cigarettes and drink Diet Coke. It's so hard to accept, as a parent, that some of the biggest, scariest things are outside your control and you can't always make it all better. Having the baby so early and nearly losing her undercut much of Caitlin's sense of confidence not only in herself but in the world.

I could only try to reassure her that she was doing her best and help to make her life easier. When I wasn't actively taking care of Caitlin or accompanying her to the hospital, I shopped and cooked and cleaned the apartment and took out the laundry. I ordered nursery items with delivery held for some time in the future. There was no room for a crib in Caitlin and Ravi's one-bedroom apartment unless they removed their bed. They had to move before they brought that baby home. And with Ravi trying to bank time at work, and Caitlin spending every minute she could with the baby, it fell to me to do all the house hunting.

Ravi taught me how to plot my route on

Google Maps when I ventured to neighborhoods with apartments that were big enough
for a family and affordable for both them
and me. Despite living in or near New York
for most of my life, I'd never even heard of,
much less been to, these neighborhoods:
Kingsbridge and Mott Haven in the Bronx,
Auburndale and Glendale in Queens,
Gravesend and Dyker Heights in Brooklyn,
Huguenot and Great Kills in Staten Island.

I took public transportation on all these
house-hunting trips, partly because it was
invariably faster than driving and partly
because I wanted to experience for myself
how long it took to get there, and how big a
pain in the ass it was.

I was in Great Kills, which I wanted to
disqualify along with Gravesend on the basis
of the names alone, when Kelsey called. It
had taken me nearly two hours to get there
from Caitlin and Ravi's apartment on the
Upper West Side, first by subway, then
across New York Harbor on the Staten
Island Ferry, and then twelve stops on the
mostly aboveground Staten Island Railway.
It didn't seem fair to have to travel that far
to see a butt-ugly house with aluminum sid-
ing and fake wood floors, only to turn
around and go all the way back. I couldn't
imagine making that round trip every day,

and from what I could see, Great Kills didn't offer any more in the way of urban sophistication than any closer and more affordable suburb.

I was nearly back at the train station when my phone buzzed. When I saw it was Kelsey, I considered letting it go to voice mail. There were only two trains an hour in the middle of the day from this station, and if I picked up the phone, I was going to miss the next one. On the other hand, if I didn't pick up, I wouldn't have a chance to talk to Kelsey again for at least the two-hour trip home and maybe longer if Caitlin was back from the hospital. I turned away from the station and answered.

I'd texted Hugo and talked on the phone to him, of course, the day after the baby was born. Kelsey had taken a little longer. It was three or four days after I returned to New York before I could bring myself to respond to her torrent of texts. *It's your show now,* I wrote. *I'm sure it will be a hit. My place is in New York with Caitlin and the baby.*

I'd been avoiding actually talking to Kelsey, though. She, along with my whole California sojourn, felt very far away. It was Before. Before Eloise. Before I became real.

"Hey," I said into the phone, bracing myself for a confrontation.

199

"Tell me about the baby," Kelsey said without preamble. "Is she beautiful?"

My knees practically buckled in relief. All I wanted at this stage was to reconnect with Kelsey as a friend and let what happened in LA stay in LA.

"Most beautiful baby ever," I said.

Eloise was starting to look more like an infant now, even sprouting a tuft of dark hair that, when the light hit it just right, had a coppery cast.

"Everything is okay?" Kelsey said. "The baby's going to be okay, Caitlin and her husband are managing?"

"They're getting there," I said. "It's been rough."

"It sounds terrifying," said Kelsey. "How are you? How's my boy Theo?"

"Oh, you mean my fur baby? He's fine. Still not human, though."

I laughed. "Don't tell him."

By this point, I had walked nearly all the way back to the house I'd looked at. It was a hot, swampy day. I'd worn a dress, thinking that would be cooler, but my thighs were chafing and the straps of my sandals were biting into my toes.

"Will you forgive me for what happened in Fernando's office?" Kelsey said. "Seriously, Liza. I'm sorry for everything. You've got to come back to the show. I cannot do this without you."

"Oh, come on. Of course you can."

I turned the corner, aiming to circle back to the train station.

"I literally can't," Kelsey said. "Hugo said he'd do the show only if you were working on it, and Stella said she'd do it only if Hugo was working on it, and if this deal falls apart, your seriously wonderful book — I mean that, Liza — will never be a TV show."

It warmed my heart hearing that Hugo had made a public stand for only doing the show if I was involved. But as I'd already told him, that wasn't enough to lure me back.

"The show you're doing is not based on my book," I told her.

"I know. You're right about all that," Kelsey said. "I told Stella and the network it's nonnegotiable: the character is in her forties, her daughter is grown-up, and she's got a younger boyfriend as well as whoever James is."

"Wow, Josh is back in it?" I said.

"Yes, I pushed for that," Kelsey said.

I had never told her that Josh was relieved not to be a character in the show. I hadn't wanted to give her the satisfaction of knowing that change worked out for the best all around.

"You might have to talk the real Josh into that," I said. "That was why he wanted the character to have his name, so he'd have some power over what they did with it. I mean, what you do with it."

"Smarter than he looks," Kelsey said. "I'll get in touch with him. He'll need to sign a life rights contract."

"Life rights? What's that?"

"When you base a character on a real person, you need to get them to sign over the right for you to use any details of their life. Life rights."

"Josh isn't going to like that, and I don't either," I said.

"Okay, whatever you want," Kelsey said. "We can have a character named Josh or we can have a younger guy with a different name. You're the author; it can be anything you say."

"Let's separate my life and the people in it from the book and the show," I said. "I wrote it as fiction, and I want it to remain fictional."

"That's fine," Kelsey said. "Your book is the show I want to do. And if we change something, I want us to change it together. I lived this with you, remember? And I want to turn it into a television show with you too."

I was a few blocks from the station. Soon, the train after the train I'd missed would be pulling in.

"I don't know, Kelsey."

"If you work with me on it, I can't guarantee that everything will go exactly the way you want, but at least you'll have a voice. You'll get your creator credit. And maybe you'll even make some money."

Money sounded good. Enough money not to live in a neighborhood that was part of New York only on a technicality.

"I can't go back to LA," I said.

"Stella said she'd shoot in New York," Kelsey said.

"What?" I stopped walking and stepped to the side so everyone heading to the station could go around me. "Why would she do that?"

"I've got this theory: I think the reason Stella suddenly wants to go to New York is because something's going on between her and Hugo."

I felt my face flush hot. "Something's going on as in something's going on?"

"Most definitely. I've heard rumors. And you can feel the heat when you're with them. I mean, can't you?"

Apparently, I wasn't able to assess the situation rationally because I was flooded with a tide of adolescent thoughts and feelings. *He likes somebody else. Everybody knows it. He was lying to me. I am such a fucking idiot.*

And then fifty-year-old Liza slapped me across the face. *You're upset because your movie star crush who wasn't even really in your life might maybe have a crush on somebody else? He said he'd only do the job if you were involved, didn't he? That might mean he's looking for an opportunity to be close again. Leverage this job into an opportunity to assess the veracity of the allegations of the affair, and rationally gauge the potential for the two of you to have a future relationship.*

*Are you fucking kidding me?* teenage Liza broke in. *You think there is any way on earth that this handsome, wonderful, rich-and-famous man would prefer you to a gorgeous movie star who is at least a surgical approximation of thirty-three? She's got the wisdom of a crone and the body of a babe, and you're just a boring old grandmother.*

"No, no, NO," I said, loudly enough that the other station-goers edged away. I turned my back to them.

Dusk was falling. Or maybe it always looked like that here.

"I can't work on the show again," I told Kelsey. Mature as I wanted to be, I was not going to have an easy time being around Hugo if he was indeed having an affair with Stella. Stella had been a nightmare before, and I had every reason to think that, cut loose from her husband and household, she might be an even bigger one in New York. Promises aside, every creative decision was effectively out of my control.

And then there was Caitlin. And Eloise. And what I'd learned was most important for me in my life.

"Okay," Kelsey said soberly. "Then there's no more show. Fernando already told me that if we don't move forward, Whipple's going to kill the whole project."

That hurt, hearing it for real. But it was the price I as a mature adult person decided I would pay. "That's too bad," I said. "But I understand."

"I guess that's it then," she said. "Are you going to break the news to Mrs. Whitney, or should I?"

Fuuuuuuuuuuuuuck. I had forgotten all about Mrs. Whitney's pivotal role — emotional, financial, and legal — in this whole enterprise. Of course she would not want the show cancelled. It might mean that Empirical would go out of business. And

I'd have to tell her — or Kelsey would do it for me — that the show wasn't happening and she was never going to earn any money on her half of the film rights because I didn't feel like spending a couple of afternoons on a television shoot.

Yeah, I wasn't going to appear before my professional goddess and do that.

Plus, I really did want to see Hugo again. Even if it was going to make me cry.

"I don't know if I can bear to tell Mrs. Whitney this isn't going to happen."

"I know," Kelsey said, her voice rich with sympathy. "I'm sure she's going to be really disappointed."

"I'm disappointed too," I said.

Oddly, this was the first time I had really let myself feel this. I'd been so busy compromising and rationalizing and defending and distancing that I hadn't spent a minute sitting with the profound disappointment of believing my book was going to be made into a television show and that maybe, just maybe, I might have a glamorous new career and make the kind of money that could change my life, and then having it all vanish.

It didn't vanish, I reminded myself: I walked away from it. Which meant I could walk back in.

"So you're making a commitment to me that you and I will set the creative course of the show, and not Stella or Fernando or anyone else?" I said.

"I swear to you, Liza. It's you and me."

I wanted to believe her. And maybe the only way to find out whether it would really go the way we wanted was to jump back in and see what happened.

"When would we start?" I asked her.

"Whenever you say. As soon as I can move everybody to New York."

"My first priority is Caitlin and the baby," I said. "My time working on the show needs to be flexible enough to take care of whatever they need from me."

I wasn't going to shunt them aside again. On the other hand, if I was working in New York and had a flexible schedule and control over my time, there was no reason I couldn't do both. Millions of women handled both a job and a family, and I wasn't the hands-on parent here. I should be able to manage it too.

"Of course," Kelsey said. "Whatever you need. Just tell me and we'll make it work."

I took a deep breath. "I want to do this," I told her. "But mostly I want my friend back."

"Oh God," Kelsey said in a rush. "I want

that too. We've always done such great work together, and you're one of my closest friends. Can we please have both?"

"I would love that," I said. "For me, that doesn't mean you need to compromise to make me happy or never disagree with me. But if there's a problem, we need to be able to talk about it with each other first."

"Agreed," said Kelsey. "Our allegiances got screwed up in LA, I think. I was caring too much about what Stella and the network wanted, and I thought you were getting too involved with Hugo."

"Right," I said.

"But now Stella and Hugo can take care of each other, and you and I will do this the way we want," Kelsey went on happily. I was happy too. Except about the Stella and Hugo part. But whatever: Kelsey was right. The important thing in the end was that she and I reclaim our working relationship and make the show we both felt good about.

"There is one other thing I need to bring up," Kelsey said. "Shooting in New York instead of LA or even someplace like Toronto is going to eat up more of our production budget. We've got to house people and we're not going to have the studio. Which means we're going to have to find ways to cut costs."

"What if we used some real locations?" I said. "Maybe Maggie would let us shoot at her loft, and we can use the Empirical Press offices."

"Ooooh, I love that," Kelsey said. "Would you ask Mrs. Whitney if she'll let us do that?"

The idea of going to her with that request rather than the news that the show was over filled me with relief and excitement.

"Absolutely," I said.

"I'll email you a location contract for her," Kelsey said. "Which reminds me: Would you also see if she has any other paperwork for us? Betty said she sent it to Whipple, but Fernando says it's not in their files."

"Of course," I said. "When do you think we'll start shooting?"

"It's going to take a while to move everyone and hire a New York crew," said Kelsey. "But we should be able to start shooting in a couple of weeks."

"I'm excited," I told her.

"I love you," Kelsey said.

I couldn't remember when I'd been so unambivalently happy to hear those words.

# SEVENTEEN

Caitlin asked me to go to the hospital to sit with the baby so she and Ravi could go apartment-hunting together. She'd heard about this place in a neighborhood they hadn't considered before, so she wanted him to look at it with her.

"Is it in Brooklyn?" I asked. I felt like I'd explored nearly every neighborhood in Brooklyn.

She shook her head no.

"Queens?"

Again, no.

"Don't tell me the Bronx."

I liked hearing her laugh.

"If you could spend the afternoon in the hospital with the peanut, that would be great," my daughter said.

Eloise was still in the neonatal intensive care unit, but she was growing quickly. Caitlin and Ravi were allowed to hold her now, but I still wasn't permitted to do anything more than gaze at her through the plexi-glass of her incubator.

I had gotten used to the routine at the hospital. I knew the people at the front desk, as well as the nurses in the NICU. Washing hands was compulsory, of course. Then you had to don a hospital gown and a cap, along with covers for your shoes. Only then were you ushered in to sit beside the incubator of the miniature human you loved.

Eloise looked bigger than when I had last seen her three days before, her skin pinker, her milky eyes half-open but unfocused. Her tuft of dark hair gave off a reddish shine and she had an adorable cleft chin, like her dad.

I put my face near the glass, even though I knew she couldn't really see me. There were tubes and monitors attached to every part of her little body. Her bare chest was no wider than my hand. I watched it rise and fall with her breath — no more scary ventilator, thank goodness — and breathed along with her, as if I were a conductor keeping her on rhythm.

There was a port in the side of the incubator you could reach through to touch her. I had seen Caitlin and Ravi do this, but since I'd only been allowed to visit for brief periods before, and always as the second or third person in the room, I hadn't been permitted to touch her.

Now, though, it was all up to me. I rubbed my hands together to make sure they were warm, then reached tentatively into the case. I touched her little hand and instantly, she wrapped her minuscule fingers around mine and hung on as if I were keeping her alive.

"Hello," I whispered. "Hello, Eloise."

"Would you like to hold her?"

It was Judy, one of the older nurses, who handled the babies as confidently as if they were loaves of bread.

"Can I?" I asked, surprised.

"The little miss is ready," Judy said. "And I bet Grandma is too."

Judy came to New York from Trinidad thirty years ago, but still spoke with a heavy, melodic accent.

When I was properly positioned on the armchair, Judy unhooked my granddaughter from her monitors, covered her hair with a tiny striped hipster beanie, and placed her against my chest with her little head right beneath my nose. I held Eloise against me, my two hands cupping her from shoulder to tucked-up toes.

"Now you are her whole world," Judy said, moving off to tend to her other charges.

Sitting there holding my newborn grand-daughter against me, her heart fluttering so close to her skin that it might almost be exposed, feeling her grow warmer as I held her, while I grew warmer myself, I felt a powerful sense of oneness with the universe. It took me back to the moment I first held Caitlin on my chest, shaking with exhaustion and weeping with joy on the delivery table.

I was only too aware how rare these moments were, how life mostly moved too quickly and insistently with children to entertain many cosmic reflections. But I remembered that first time I held my child and perceived the gravity of our eternal connection, the way that sometimes in an airplane you suddenly understand that you are thousands of feet above the ground, or when someone you love dies and you realize you will never speak to them again. That feeling is too big and too terrifying to hold on to for long, and with children everything is constantly changing, every single day.

I never thought I would feel that profound first connection with a newborn again. After my miscarriages, I came to accept that there would be no more babies in my future. It almost felt as if I'd made that choice.

213

But I'd been wrong. There was a new baby in my future, a child who would be in my life forever, and she was sleeping warm in my arms right now.

Caitlin was feeling stronger, and so I decided everyone would be more comfortable if I moved to Maggie's. Asking Maggie if I could stay there was a formality; she always said yes immediately and told me that I didn't need to ask. But this time she hesitated for long enough that it was weird.

"What's wrong?" I asked.

I hadn't seen or even talked to Maggie since that first night at the hospital. We'd exchanged a few texts and emails, quick cursory updates on Caitlin and the baby. Maggie had, I knew, been to the hospital a handful of times, but never when I was there. I hadn't thought anything of it. When I wasn't helping Caitlin and looking at apartments on the far edges of New York, I was comatose on Caitlin and Ravi's couch.

"We should talk," Maggie said.

"What do you mean? What happened?"

"Let's go for a walk," Maggie said.

We met at the Fourteenth Street stairway to the High Line. It was a rare beautiful New York summer day, not too hot, not too humid, the sky as blue and cloudless as

California's. Maggie was wearing a jumpsuit with the sleeves and legs cut off and blotches of paint and plaster all over it. The Hauser & Wirth show had opened the door to invitations from galleries and museums around the world. Frankie, who had summers off, had taken the kids to the beach to give Maggie the time and the solitude to make some new work.

We climbed the steep iron stairway, me behind Maggie, feeling as if I were being led up to the hangman's scaffold. What was such a big deal she had to meet me at this special place to discuss it in person? But by the time we reached the elevated pedestrian walkway, where the air was fresher and the chaos of the city seemed far away, I'd gained some perspective.

"Oh, I get it," I said, vastly relieved at what I believed was my realization of why Maggie wanted to talk to me. "You've finally got the house to yourself and you need the time alone to work. I totally understand. I'll find somewhere else to stay."

I had already jumped ahead in my mind to the possibilities: stick it out on Caitlin's couch for a bit longer, stay in Mrs. Whitney's spare room over on York Avenue. If worse came to worse, I could camp with one of my old mom friends in New Jersey, but as time went on and our kids left home, there were fewer and fewer of those.

"This isn't about you staying with me," Maggie said.

I wasn't sure if this was good news or bad news.

"I want to talk about the day your grand-daughter was born."

"I was already on my way back to New York when you called me," I said, already defensive. "I told you that, right?"

That day spent jetting across the country, not knowing whether my grandchild was going to live or die, seemed even crazier in retrospect against the contrast of this pastoral corner of the city, with its potted greenery and ambling tourists.

"Yeah, you told me that, but just because you were coming home of your own volition a month after you said you would doesn't mean you were doing the right thing."

"I was doing my best," I said. "Nobody thought Caitlin was going to go into labor that day. She was only thirty-two weeks pregnant."

"But I told you two weeks before that to come home. It was like you cared more about running around with your Hollywood friends, going to parties and getting high, than being with your kid."

I stopped walking and looked at Maggie. People streamed around us, the sun shone down, but it was like I was being mugged by my own feelings. I had not been so angry at anyone since the day I left Josh.

"That is really unfair," I said. "You were the one who made a big case about me taking that job and going out there! You almost made it sound like it would be antifeminist treason to turn it down in favor of staying in New York with Caitlin, which if you remember was what I wanted to do."

"I remember you *saying* you were going to stay in New York with Caitlin; I don't know about *wanting* to. You seemed to want to do nothing but party once you got there."

"I was working my ass off," I said. "Was I supposed to be miserable every minute?"

"You were supposed to get your work done and come home," Maggie said. "You were acting like a college kid on spring break, having so much fun you missed the first day of classes."

"I am going to regret for the rest of my life that I wasn't here with Caitlin that day," I said. "Why do you have to make me feel even worse about it?"

"I don't think you realize how scared I was, Liza! Ravi took forever to get there, the baby was in distress, and they were asking me to make decisions about Caesareans and all this medical stuff, and you had shut down your fucking phone!"

"I'm sorry," I said quietly. I *was* unambivalently sorry about turning off my phone that day, not only because Maggie couldn't reach me when she needed me, but because I wished I'd dealt with Kelsey and the conflict over the show more directly.

"But you know, once you did reach me, you could have told me what was going on. You didn't have to keep holding all of that responsibility by yourself."

"I didn't tell you because I love you," Maggie said. "I was trying to protect you from worrying when you were too far away to do anything."

I tilted my head and studied Maggie. "Or maybe you wanted it. Maybe you wanted to prove you were a better mother than me."

"Being a good mother means being there for your kids," Maggie said piously, "and you haven't been there for a really long time."

"I am there for Caitlin, but she's an adult, not a child," I said. "I was there for her full-time when she was growing up, while you built your career, and now that I'm trying to build mine, you can help me without

218

making me feel like I'm failing as a mother."

We both stopped talking then, but began walking, at a more meditative pace. I was really glad that we were on the High Line rather than down on the streets. The High Line seemed magically to adjust, depending on your mood: It could feel calm or exciting or novel or secure; it had been all those things to us on this single walk. I'd felt freer than I might have down below to express my anger, but now all my angry feelings flooded out of me like, well, like your water breaking when you go into labor. I felt so exhausted, suddenly, I could have lain down on one of the wooden benches and fallen asleep.

"I'm sorry," Maggie said finally. "I don't think you failed as a mother. I was just so fucking terrified."

"Oh God, me too," I said.

"If I lost either one of them," she said, "I could never forgive myself."

We kept walking.

"I would have killed you," I told her.

"You wouldn't have been able to," Maggie said. "Because I would have already killed myself."

"I actually prayed on the plane, the entire five hours. All these prayers from Saint Cassian's came back to me."

Maggie linked her arm through mine and tugged me close. "I want to hear about the private plane that Hugo Fielding hired for you," she said. "But that's a two-martini discussion. Let's go home."

"Does that mean I can stay with you?" I asked.

"Of course you can stay with me," she said. "But I want sordid details."

I wished the details I had were more sordid. Or maybe less sordid. Right now, Hugo was marooned somewhere uncomfortably in the middle — he'd become my favorite masturbation fantasy, but one I felt too guilty about to enjoy.

"Hugo and I had a moment in LA, but nothing happened, not really. And now Kelsey says Stella's agreed to shoot the show in New York because she's having an affair with Hugo and wants to be far from home with him."

"Shut *up!*" Maggie said. "Do you think it's true?"

"I don't know. That night at the mushroom party, I felt something genuine from him. But what Kelsey says makes so much sense, much more sense than him falling for me."

"Who cares?" said Maggie. "I think you should at least fuck his brains out."

Anyone watching us would have guessed we were discussing roast chicken recipes and Oprah's latest book club pick. Something I was discovering about being middle-aged and looking it was that people always assumed that whatever you were thinking about or talking about was boring to the point of being stultifying. Which could be a big advantage, I supposed, if you were a CIA agent or drug smuggler.

"I could get hurt," I said.

"You could have fun."

"What if he's really with Stella?"

"Then it's on him to tell you. And her. Plus she, might I remind you, is married to someone else. You and Hugo are both single people."

"He's an actor," I pointed out. "It might all be fake."

"And a person who would fake anything is someone you need to stay away from," Maggie said placidly.

It took me an embarrassingly long time to realize she was talking about me.

# EIGHTEEN

Kelsey landed in New York and hit the ground running. She had — *we* had — less than a month to get the pilot shot. That included hiring a crew, arranging locations, producing costumes. One unexpected benefit of agreeing to work on the show again was that it came with a free place to live — the second bedroom in the apartment Kelsey rented — which meant that Maggie's poor nanny could have her room back.

"You're not a New York resident and you don't have a place here, so you qualify for an out-of-town stipend," Kelsey said. "Just like me."

The place Kelsey found was a corporate apartment, bland but comfortable, located downtown on the river, facing New Jersey. Hello, New Jersey. I wish I knew how to quit you.

Stella and Hugo were slated to arrive on Sunday night, and we were scheduled to start shooting on Monday. The very first scene, when Alice gets hired at Gentility Press, was going to be shot at . . . Empirical Press. How meta was that?

Mrs. Whitney had been delighted to have us shoot at Empirical on one condition: She got to play herself.

"I can't screw it up too badly," she said. "This is my shot at immortality."

Kelsey and I assured her that she was already immortal, but that we couldn't imagine anyone who would bring more to the role of Mrs. Whitney. She waived the location fee, but insisted that all the books on the shelves and desks at the fictional Gentility Press be those published by the real Empirical Press. Just when you thought Mrs. Whitney was a publisher solely because she loved books, she showed you how she turned that passion into a business.

It was bizarre walking into Empirical Press after the set designer and decorator got through with it: Though it felt like a hundred years ago that I'd worked there, seeing the place done up to look exactly as it had back then also made it seem as if no time at all had passed.

The velvet sofa looked comfortably luxurious rather than tattered; the wooden desks were polished, with books and papers stacked neatly — too neatly — on top. The seats were all occupied by extras, looking extraordinarily well groomed and elegantly dressed, more like people who worked in a fashion designer's showroom than like real editors.

I was on the editors' side of the room, encouraging everyone to roll up their sleeves and slump their shoulders, when there was a rise in the timbre of the voices of a hundred people, and a heightened vibration in the room. I looked up to see Hugo and Stella making their entrances, double-kissing people hello, waving across the room. The stars had arrived.

Hugo caught me staring and broke into a big grin, waving wildly. I gave him a small, tight smile back, the kind of smile that said, *Nice to see you, but I hear you're in love with somebody else, asshole.* That apparently was not the message Hugo got, because he seemed to be headed across the room toward me.

I quickly whipped around and began messing up one of the too-tidy desks, spreading the books around and actually throwing a sheaf of papers up in the air. Then I noticed the poor extra who was sitting at the desk staring at me in horror, probably wondering whether he should call security. I tried to gather the papers back together but instead shuffled them onto the floor. When I finally turned around again in mortification, I found that Hugo had apparently not been aiming to see me at all but was hunched over the script with Kelsey, who'd been dressing in head-to-toe black since she'd landed at JFK, and Mrs. Whitney, looking even more slender and glamorous than usual.

Kelsey walked away, but Mrs. Whitney and Hugo kept talking. I really wanted to know what they were talking about, but not as much as I wanted to stand back and watch them talking. Hugo was flirting with Mrs. Whitney, I realized, quite outrageously, and she was flirting even more outrageously back.

*You are even more gorgeous than you look in the movies,* I imagined her saying.

*You are a fascinating woman,* I imagined Hugo saying in return. *I would love to go out with you, but then again, I'd go out with anybody.*

*Liza seemed to actually believe you were interested in her,* my now fictional Mrs. Whitney said.

*I'm interested in every woman!* fictional Hugo said. *It's all a lie!*

Then as if from a cloud of smoke, there

was Stella, draping her long blond arm over Hugo's shoulder, taking an ostentatious sniff of Hugo's neck, and finally bursting into musical laughter. Her hair looked like Sleeping Beauty's.

"Liza!" Real Stella squealed with delight upon spotting me and teetered over on her four-inch heels to give me one of her trademark four-cheek kisses.

"You're here!" I said.

"I have to follow my passion," said Stella. Ha!

I hadn't quite looked at Hugo yet. But that didn't stop him from crossing the room and giving me an enormous hug. I mean really enormous.

"So excited to be here," he said.

"Where are you staying?" I asked, pulling away so I wouldn't feel quite so much of his excitement. Or my own.

"We have a place uptown, on Central Park West," Stella said. "Where John Lennon died."

"You have a place in the Dakota?"

"It's only a four-bedroom," she said.

"Do you have the kids with you?" I asked Stella.

"Oh *no,* it wouldn't be fair to drag them across the country," Stella said. "Kelsey said she didn't bring Theo either."

226

"Theo's a dog," I pointed out.

"Same thing," said Stella.

Actually, no, though it was usually the dog owner not the mother who needed to be disabused of that notion.

"So are you two," I said, pointing from Stella to Hugo and back again, "*both* staying at your place at the Dakota?"

Hugo gave me a strange look. "I'm in those corporate places downtown, near you," he said.

"Though he *could* stay over," Stella said. "Anytime he wants."

"Your husband wouldn't mind?" I asked.

"Are you kidding? He'd cum at his desk just hearing about it."

That comment propelled me out of reality for so long that I only came back to the room when I heard Kelsey clapping her hands. She might have been clapping for a long time.

"Are we ready to shoot this thing?" she said.

Shooting a television show is one of those occupations that involves dozens of grown-up people standing around looking like they're not doing anything, except if you're *really* standing around not doing anything, you're in the way.

227

I'm not saying I had nothing to do. I'm saying I didn't even have a clue what the possibilities were. Kelsey was the show-runner, which meant she was the final on-set authority on everything. The director, the cinematographer, the AD, the production designer, even the actors — they all turned to her. So my job, theoretically, was to consult with her if she wasn't sure on some creative decision and to handle any rewrites that might become necessary in the course of shooting. Because even though you've rewritten something twenty-five times, you may get all the actors saying their lines at a location and the words simply don't sound right, as if the lights and the camera caused some alchemic reaction.

Mostly, though, I stood there with my arms crossed over my chest, shifting to the left and to the right, trying to stay out of everyone's way, while also trying to look serious and purposeful. We were shooting a scene early in the script where Alice comes in for her job interview as her fake millennial self and fears she'll be exposed when Mrs. Whitney interrupts the interview. Alice worked for the same company twenty-five years ago; will Mrs. Whitney remember Alice and ruin the whole enterprise before it gets off the ground?

Spoiler alert: Mrs. Whitney doesn't remember, and Alice gets the job.

Before Kelsey called "Action!", Stella, posing as Alice posing as a twenty-six-year-old, came into the office where we were shooting — Mrs. Whitney's own white-themed office, as it turned out — for a lighting check. She was dressed in a hot-pink patent leather skirt that barely covered her ass cheeks and a tank top that said *Jersey Shore.*

I leaned over and whispered in Kelsey's ear, "Seriously?"

Kelsey called the wardrobe person over, who said the shirt was Stella's idea. Then Kelsey talked to Stella, who changed into a white tee shirt.

It was a single-camera show, which meant that every shot had to be staged and filmed on its own: There weren't multiple cameras shooting from different angles, catching every dimension of a scene at once.

Instead we filmed Stella lying by omission to the young HR woman about her age and experience, bright innocence on her face, then shot the HR woman nodding and questioning, *then* shot Mrs. Whitney entering the office and shaking Stella's hand, and then filmed Hugo interrupting them all. The lingering, interested glance between him

229

and Stella — *I see you, and I like what I see, though I know I'm not supposed to* — had to be shot in close-up an excruciating number of times. They didn't even have to say anything, just lock eyes and shake hands for a few beats too long, but Stella kept giggling in the middle of the handshake, or dropping her head on Hugo's shoulder, and once even entwined him in a big kiss.

I finally couldn't watch it anymore and tiptoed off the set, slipping into the little employee lunchroom that was tucked back near the elevators. I was counting on it being the one place in the entire office that had not been discovered by the crew, and I was right. It was deserted, except for one person: Mrs. Whitney, looking very out of place sitting on a black plastic chair in her white Chanel suit with her Ferragamos off and her feet up.

"Having fun?" I said.

She startled and set her feet on the ground. "Oh, Liza," she said, her hand at her throat. "Do you need me for something? I didn't mean to sneak away; I just needed a bit of a break."

It was late afternoon by this time, but she'd opened up Empirical's offices for us at seven a.m.

"No, that's all right," I reassured her. "I

230

was just looking for a little escape myself."

"Keep me company, then," Mrs. Whitney said, patting the plastic chair beside her. "We can catch up on all the gossip."

I'd filled her in on my grandchild and outlined the progress of the show when I'd arranged to use the office as a location. But I didn't think that was the kind of gossip she was interested in.

"Hugo Fielding seems very nice," she said. "Very admiring of you."

"He's very admiring of Stella," I said.

Things did seem different between the two of them here than they had been in LA. Not only physically closer, but freer, it seemed, which made perfect sense. Here they could do whatever they pleased.

"I wouldn't be concerned about that," Mrs. Whitney said.

"Really?" I said, surprised. "Why do you say that?"

"There's something artificial about it," she said. "It hits one almost like a bad smell."

Had I just not gotten close enough to detect it? They certainly smelled pretty warm and cozy every time I'd been near them.

"Maybe I'm just disappointed that the lovely Sutton Foster didn't get to play the part," continued Mrs. Whitney. "Did I tell you she wrote me?"

"Sutton Foster wrote you? No!"

"A lovely handwritten note on the most beautiful stationery. She told me how much she loved the book and admired me as a character and a woman. We met for tea at The Carlyle before one of her shows. You know she plays often at the Café Carlyle."

"Right across from Bemelmans," I said.

"She would have made a lovely Alice," said Mrs. Whitney.

"What might have been," I said.

"Well, I've got a wonderful new friend out of it," said Mrs. Whitney. "We'll have to all get together one day."

That idea thrilled me more than even the prospect of first meeting Hugo. I was about to press Mrs. Whitney to make a date when I noticed how tired she looked around the eyes. She'd already shot her scenes; she didn't need to be here any longer. We could talk about our celebrity friends another time.

"Unless Kelsey still needs you for something, you can go home if you want," I told her.

"I have to stay here to lock up."

"Kelsey and I can do that," I said.

She looked at me in surprise.

"We did it together plenty of times," I

reminded her.

She laughed. "That's true. So much has changed, I'd forgotten that you two practically ran the place at one time."

"We always knew you were there to save us if we screwed up."

"I have the feeling you'll do just fine without me this time."

I noticed for the first time, as she left the office, how much frailer she looked, thin and small. Rather than the boss I'd always seen as all-powerful, she seemed almost like a child now. I wanted to protect her, but at the same time, I wished she'd come back and keep protecting me.

At the end of the day, as we were packing up to leave, I got a text from Hugo.

*Drink?*

I looked up. He was standing across the room. He smiled and shrugged.

I shook my head no and went back to packing.

My phone chimed again.

*Late dinner?*

*Too tired,* I typed.

The three dots danced on the screen for a moment. I looked over, but he was staring at his phone, typing, deleting, typing, deleting.

233

I slipped my phone in my back pocket and went back to packing. I wanted to leave the place in perfect shape for Mrs. Whitney, as if we'd never been there. And I didn't want to get together with Hugo until I'd had a chance to judge for myself whether the rumors I'd heard about him and Stella were true.

Then suddenly he was in front of me.

"Are you angry?" he said.

"No, why would I be angry?"

"It seems like you're avoiding me."

Part of me wanted to confront him, to ask him pointblank if he was with Stella, so I would know what was what and where I stood. Where he stood. But he could say anything. What mattered was what he did.

"Just busy," I said.

"You're from New York, right?" he said. "I was hoping you could show me around."

"I'd love to," I said. "But everything's so crazy right now. Maybe you and Stella can go exploring together."

"Ha!" he said. "The only thing Stella likes to do is shop."

"What do you want to do?"

"If I'm on my own, I'd say go to the theater," he said. "My dream has always been to be on Broadway."

"Really?" I said, surprised and amused.

"Like, singing and dancing?"

"No, I see myself in some tragic drama like *Long Day's Journey* or *Death of a Salesman.*"

"So why haven't you done that?" I said.

He shrugged. "Nobody asked me. I guess no one thought my work in *My Other Honeymoon* demonstrated that I had the emotional depth to rip my heart out onstage in front of a live audience."

"And do you?" I said, half-teasing.

"Nobody is in a better position to judge that than you," he said.

"Me?" I said. "Why me?"

"You're the one I've been ripping my heart out in front of," he said.

He looked hard at me then, as if asking me to reassure him that there was something emotional between us, that the connection had been real.

"I'm sure you'd be great at theater," I told him. "You should pursue that after we wrap."

It may not have been a marriage proposal, nor was it a total fuck you, but it was the best I could offer at that moment.

"I wish I could," he said, "but Stella wants me to commit to this indie she's putting together based on the life of her surf instructor, Tane. Have you met him? Anyway, that shoot starts in Hawaii right after we wrap."

"That will be nice for you and Stella," I said coolly.

I wrapped one of the books on the table in packing paper, knowing full well that it wasn't going anywhere, that it belonged right there on the table.

"I know Stella can be a pain," he said, "but we've known each other a long time and I really love her."

"That's what I've heard," I said.

"She can be ridiculous, but she listens to reason. She agreed in the end to come out here and do this your way."

"I heard that was thanks to you."

"I had something to do with it," he admitted.

"You two seem very close," I said.

"We are close! That's why we wanted to work together. We're the best of friends."

He kept standing there with a big boyish grin on his face. Did he not know what I was getting at? Was he telling me something in a veiled way that I failed to understand? Fuck veiled. My year-long masquerade to the contrary, veiled was so not my style.

"I heard there's more than that between you and Stella," I found myself saying.

"What do you mean?"

"I heard you two were having an affair."

I stopped all my fussing around and looked at him directly then. I wanted to stare him in the eye and judge whether he was telling me the truth.

"Liza, I swear to you that Stella and I are not having an affair," Hugo said, looking straight at me, in the voice I trusted.

I felt so much better. For about ten seconds. Until I realized I was not sure whether I believed him. Why was the truth always so much more elusive and complicated than it was supposed to be?

# NINETEEN

When I saw Josh's name on my phone, I
nearly didn't pick up. But I hadn't picked
up the last three times he called, and I felt
too guilty to blow him off again. I could
plead work and baby and all-around life
craziness, but the truth was that I was
scared to see him again. I couldn't handle
the push-pull of our inevitable attraction,
coupled with my conviction that we were
never ever getting back together.

"Hey," I answered, already formulating
my apologies and excuses.

"I broke up with Zen," he blurted.

"Oh no, Josh. What happened?"

"It just . . . I think if you're going to get
married, you shouldn't have any doubts,
right?" he said.

With David, I'd been flooded with doubts,
but dismissed every one of them. It was
normal to be jittery, I'd told myself. We'd
work out our problems over time. I'd been

quaking so hard on my father's arm as he walked me down the aisle that he'd leaned over and said in my ear, "You don't have to do this."

I'd often wished I could go back and lift myself right out of the picture at that wedding, except then I wouldn't have Caitlin. And having her had been worth everything else.

"You're right," I said. "You shouldn't be questioning whether you want to do it."

"I never had doubts about you," he said.

"Except whether you should marry someone you couldn't have kids with."

"You're the one who had doubts about that."

I hadn't had doubts. I was sure I wanted to marry him, and then when he told me he wanted kids after all, I was sure I didn't.

"You know, you've been feeling unsure about this relationship with Zen ever since we started talking again," I said. "Maybe it's time for you to let it go."

Kelsey, who had been in the shower, walked into the living room of our corporate flat.

"Time for who to let what go?" she said, rubbing a towel over her wet hair.

*Josh,* I mouthed.

"Hi, Josh!" she sang out, and then contin-

239

ued on her way into her bedroom at the far end of the hall.

"Kelsey and I had a good talk," Josh said.

Josh had agreed there could be a character in the show based on the Josh character in the book, as long as Josh the character bore no resemblance to Josh the person, apart from their very common first name. Kelsey and I agreed we could live with that and figured that since the pilot script was already written, we'd work out the character of new Josh if we actually went to series. We could base *that* character on Kelsey's ideal man instead of mine.

"Yeah, I'm glad we worked that out."

After resisting the idea for so long, even Stella was suddenly enthusiastic about the new re-envisioned Josh. She joked that maybe he could be like her surf instructor Tane, though Tane was unwittingly already the model for the character Mrs. Whitney was going to run away with as well as the subject of Stella's biopic. He was apparently a very inspiring guy.

"Listen, Liza, can we get together?" Josh said. "I really need a friend right now."

You know when you really want to say no but you also know you can't? This was one of those times for me. I did not want to be the one to comfort him after his breakup. I also did not want to change back out of my pajamas. But Josh was one of the people I cared the most about in the world. He must really need to talk to me if he picked up the phone and called me when I hadn't been returning his messages. The idea of turning him down made me feel like too big a shit.

So I agreed, and then sat there paralyzed on the couch, staring at the floor and dreading the hours ahead. I was still sitting there when Kelsey walked back into the living room, fastening a large pearl earring in one ear. She was dressed in her New York evening uniform of short black skirt, high-heeled black sandals, and silky black shirt.

"What's with all the black?" I asked her.

"It's my sophisticated New York look," she said happily. "I think it's working: Guys like me better here."

"Are you going out on a date?" I asked.

"No, I'm going to try out this new app that helps you hook up with people in your immediate vicinity," Kelsey said.

"Like, you and the guy on the other end of the bar connect by app and have sex in the bathroom?"

"How did having sex in the bathroom get to be a thing?" Kelsey said. "I mean, a cab, a restaurant booth maybe . . ."

"A restaurant booth?" I gasped.

"But public bathroom. That's just dirty, and not in a good way."

"Want to try out the app at the Jane? I told Josh I'd meet him there. He broke up with Zen."

"This is your moment," Kelsey said.

"I don't want it to be. Will you come along with me as a favor?" I asked her. "It will help establish that he and I are in the friend zone."

Josh was already sitting at the bar, nursing some kind of strong-looking cocktail, when we arrived. He looked as handsome as ever, perched there all alone. When we all used to come to this place, it was always packed, but tonight the bar stools on either side of Josh were free.

Josh lit up when he caught sight of me across the room, then frowned when he spotted Kelsey, then smiled again when he realized it was Kelsey.

"Hello, stranger." Kelsey gave Josh a big hug.

Josh and Kelsey had been friendly apart from me, but they had also maintained a respectful distance. Kelsey claimed that Girl Code required that female friends not get too close, physically or emotionally, to each other's boyfriends, even the exes.

"Hey, I think this is where I met you for the very first time," Josh told her.

Kelsey looked quizzical. "Really? I don't remember."

"Yeah, you were with that really straight dude you used to date, a banker or a hedge fund manager or something."

"Thad."

"Poor Thad," I said.

"Yeah," said Josh. "I heard about what happened. It was awful."

"That kind of thing shouldn't happen to anybody," Kelsey said. "But that doesn't take away from the fact that he was a jerk."

"Okay, yes, thank you. He was a jerk, especially to Liza. I think she brought me along the first night for protection."

"Protection?" Kelsey said, casting a little smile and a wry glance toward me. *You haven't changed much,* she seemed to be saying.

"Thad was always suspicious about my age," I said. "I thought if he saw my young boyfriend, he'd believe I was young."

"I do remember thinking you were hot," Kelsey told Josh.

"I'm not feeling so hot tonight," he said.

Josh was usually a beer drinker — or a weed smoker — but we supplemented the Old-Fashioned he'd been nursing with three shots of whiskey, lined up on the bar.

"I know this probably doesn't help right now," I said, "but it hurts even when it's the right thing to do."

"I did love her," he said.

"Yeah," I said. "But you can love somebody and still decide you can't be together."

I wondered if he understood that I was talking about him and me.

"What if I never meet anybody else?" he said.

"Are you kidding?" said Kelsey. "I've got this new app that could probably find you ten women in this very bar tonight who would have your baby."

"Tinder?" said Josh.

Kelsey gave him a pitying look.

"Poor boy is stuck back in 2017," Kelsey said.

The two of them bent their heads over Kelsey's app, which seemed as effective as cocktail wieners on a fishing line. Only a few minutes in, Kelsey was trading messages with a man at the far end of the bar.

"Okay, Julian," she said. "I'm going in. Josh, there's a whole wonderful world of baby-ready women out there dying to meet you. Liza, I'll see you on the set early tomorrow morning."

And then she left us alone.

■ ■ ■ ■

Josh wasn't the only one feeling a buzz by the time we left the Jane. I gave him a hug goodbye on the sidewalk, trying not to hold it too long.

"Call me tomorrow and let me know how you're doing," I said.

I turned to walk away but he said, "I'll walk you."

"It's okay; I'm fine," I said.

Even when you're alone late at night in New York, you're surrounded by hundreds of people.

"Can I please walk you?" he said.

I held back for another minute, and then I caved. I thought of Mrs. Whitney saying that this was it, now is all we have, and I thought this was it with Josh. I'd had him like this all the time for a long time, and then I didn't have him at all, and now for this one moment I had him again. *Let it happen,* I told myself. *See what you feel.*

We were walking right next to each other, so close we could feel each other's heat, but I edged closer and slipped my arm through his. I caught a strong scent of Old Spice, the deodorant he'd first started using in junior high. He held up the fact that he still

245

used it as a testament to his sense of loyalty and devotion.

We walked companionably through the streets of the Village and Chelsea as we had so many times before. It felt eerily as if it were three years ago, and we were together, and in love, and nothing had ever come between us. I was living my current life instead of analyzing my old life or trying to create my new life. Infinite bliss, according to Buddha: I wanted what I had.

In front of my building, he kissed me. I responded as if it were a basic goodnight kiss at first, keeping myself in check, but I found myself melting into the kiss, into him. And feeling this turned on by him was such a precariously small step from falling back in love with him.

"I love you," he murmured.

Which made me melt further.

Until I imagined tomorrow morning. Tomorrow morning, we'd get up, tickled by what had happened, abashed, intrigued, excited, afraid, ecstatic. Our morning routine would be cozy and comfortable, like a favorite old sweater you find in the back of your closet and wear everywhere until you realize it's got holes all over it.

"You can't love me," I said.

Even though, of course, I loved him too.

"I will always love you," he murmured.

But feeling did not have to lead to action. It did not have to mean that you changed your life.

"Josh," I said. "Stop. I love you too. But we can't do this. I can't do this."

"It's always been you and me, Liza," he said. "No matter what else happens, we keep coming back to each other."

"But we have to stop doing that every time the world tilts on its axis and we feel sad or scared or overwhelmed. We cling to each other, and it feels good until we realize this isn't what we really want."

"I want you," he said.

We weren't touching now but standing awkwardly apart on the sidewalk.

"You want my company, you want my support, and you can have that," I told him. "But we can't be together again. You have to be free to have kids, not have kids, whatever, but to explore that with partners who are open to that possibility. And I need to be free too."

To do what? I wasn't sure. But something that didn't involve raising a family.

"I always thought there would be one more time," he said lamely.

I wasn't sure, in that moment, whether he was talking about one more time with me, or Zen, or expressing what most of us feel at the end of everything: surprised that there will not be just one more time. That's why death is so hard, or at least it was for me when my parents and my brother died. The absoluteness of that ending is so stunning, such an outrage. With everything living, "once more" is always technically a chance. It's so hard to grasp the possibility of "never again."

# TWENTY

Hugo texted me on Sunday morning and asked if I wanted to do something.

*With you?* I texted back.

*No, with my mother,* he wrote.

I didn't reply for so long that he finally texted back, *Joking.*

*Funny,* I typed.

*???*

*Dinner plans,* I wrote.

That was true. Kelsey and I were invited to Maggie's.

*Me too,* he wrote. *But free earlier. Meet downstairs at noon?*

I still wasn't used to thinking of him existing only one block away from me. I was much more comfortable imagining him on the other side of the country, or at least the other side of town.

*I need to see that Dancing Chicken,* he typed.

I vaguely remembered mentioning the

Dancing Chicken the night of my mushroom trip.

*OK,* I typed, and then quickly ran to wash and blow-dry my hair.

I'd been keeping an eye on him and Stella, and they seemed as close with each other as ever. But no closer. Keeping my distance from Hugo was not going to help clarify things, I rationalized. Plus, what harm could it do to go see a Dancing Chicken.

Hugo and I walked down Broadway, nearly deserted on Sunday morning, toward where the chicken held court in a gaming arcade. I explained to Hugo that when my father first took my brother and me to see the chicken, it just hopped around — thus the appellation Dancing Chicken — but over time it upped its game, literally, and began playing tic-tac-toe. I used to take my competition with the chicken very seriously, practicing with my father at home in preparation for the next round. I could never figure out why that damn chicken kept beating me. I got As in school; I was first in my class! Was it possible that a chicken was cleverer than me? It honestly did not occur to me until I reconnected with the chicken when I moved to New York after college that the game might be rigged, or that the poor chicken was being electric shocked.

Hugo found this story touching.

"You're very innocent," he said.

"I was back then."

"You still are."

"Oh, come on," I said, surprised and nearly insulted.

"Maybe *innocent* isn't the word I'm looking for," he said. "Guileless? Open?"

I couldn't help but laugh. "Remember, you're talking about the woman who lied to her boss, her boyfriend, and her best work friend about her entire identity."

"Not your entire identity," Hugo said. "Only your age."

"That involved changing my hair, wearing different clothes. Drinking tequila shots. Saying *sick* instead of *great*."

"Surface details," Hugo said. "People dye their hair and get Botox and have plastic surgery and wear Spanx all the time to appear younger. You're not allowed to ask someone's age at a job interview, and most people choose not to tell. So what makes them so different from you?"

"You're right," I told Hugo. "Everybody tries to look younger all the time, and somehow we think that's totally fine, while we'd be horrified if people were buying billions of dollars of products designed to make them look whiter or more male."

251

"You sound like a millennial," Hugo said teasingly.

"I liked being a millennial," I told him. "It made me a more sensitive old lady."

"You're not old."

"I'm turning fifty in December."

"I'm fifty-seven."

"Wow," I said, amused. His official bio, which I'd googled and reread a couple dozen times now, had him as fifty-three.

By that time, we were in Chinatown, but the chicken was not where I remembered, or anywhere else in the maze of streets below Canal. I finally ducked into Wo Hop, where my father always took us to eat after our chicken games, and asked a waiter who looked old enough to have worked there when I was a little girl.

The chicken had been rescued about twenty years before, he told us, so we did the only logical thing and ate lunch at Wo Hop. Then I guided Hugo to the East Village, where I'd lived right out of college. We had a cappuccino at Veniero's and moved on to an egg cream at Gem Spa and capped that off with a beer at McSorley's, all remnants of the New York I'd known my entire life.

The thing that tickled Hugo most was that no one seemed to recognize him. If they did, they didn't let on, absorbed in their companions or their phones. He started the day cloaked in a baseball hat and sunglasses, which looked ridiculous in the subway. He got less attention when he finally took them off.

I looked at my watch: nearly six. "I've got to go," I told him.

"Who are you having dinner with?" he asked.

"My friend Maggie."

"Ah, the famous Maggie," he said. "I still haven't met her."

"I'd invite you, but you said you had a date."

"I made that up. I thought you were having dinner with Josh, so I didn't want to sound like a loser."

I hesitated only a moment before texting Maggie to say I was bringing a friend to dinner. I didn't tell her it was Hugo. I knew she'd freak out and probably try to both cook twelve extra dishes and change into a flowing gown and high heels, all in the twenty minutes it took us to walk from the East Village to her place.

I let myself into Maggie's with the key I'd never returned and took in the regular Sunday dinner scene: Kelsey cursing as she retrieved a tray of charred and smoking cupcakes from the oven, a screaming Celia and Edie chasing Ollie around the loft, and Maggie nestling little mounds of cheese and spinach into patches of homemade ravioli dough.

Hugo trailed behind me as I crossed the room to hug Maggie and Kelsey, who was muttering curses as she dumped her cupcakes in the trash. She caught sight of Hugo before Maggie did and seemed unexpectedly rattled by his presence.

"What are you doing here?" Kelsey said.

It was only then that Maggie saw him.

"Wow," Maggie said. "You look so much like . . ."

"Maggie, this is Hugo Fielding," I said.

"Fuck me," said Maggie. She dropped the ravioli she'd been working on and, wiping her hands on the seat of her jeans, half ran across the loft and took Hugo's hand in hers. "May I just say that I've always been in love with you and I knew that one day we'd be together."

Hugo burst out laughing and threw his arms around her.

"I'm so happy to finally meet you," he said.

"How about a Manhattan?" said Maggie.

"I love you," said Hugo.

"Except you have to wait a minute, be-

254

cause my spouse, Frankie — well, soon-to-be ex-spouse, once I leave them for you — ran out to get cherries."

"Can't drink a Manhattan without cherries," Hugo said.

"It's all about the cherries," Maggie said. "And the booze."

"I didn't know you two were spending the day together," Kelsey said.

She seemed nervous. Or maybe annoyed that I was with Hugo after she'd warned me so many times not to date him? But this wasn't a date. This was two people out together, having fun.

"When you said you were bringing someone, I expected to see Josh," Maggie said to me.

"No, I invited Josh," said Kelsey, without quite meeting my eye. "He's so lonely since the breakup."

That was when the doorbell rang.

I was glad I had a tiny bit of advance warning before encountering Josh at the door. It felt awkward after what happened between us the other night. But Josh didn't seem awkward. He'd spent more time at Maggie's over the past few years than I had, I reminded myself.

He recognized Hugo instantly and heartily shook his hand. "I've heard a lot about you," he said.

"And I've heard a lot about you," said Hugo. "Or should I say, about Josh the character. I feel like I know everything about you after reading the book twice and working on the show these past weeks."

Josh sent me a quick smile. "Liza doesn't know all my secrets," he said.

The door opened and in walked Frankie, bearing a loaf of Italian bread and the world's tiniest brown paper bag, presumably containing the all-important cherries. They kissed Maggie and said a hearty hello to Josh.

"Frankie, this is Hugo," I said.

Frankie shook Hugo's hand without really looking at him. "Good to meet you. So listen to this saga. I went to the liquor store over on Delancey, but they only had the bright red cherries. Didn't they outlaw those in like 1968? That's how long this jar was probably on the shelf. And then Reggio's was out of Italian bread, so I decided to go up to Vesuvio's for the bread, and while I was there go to that fancy liquor store on Astor Place for the right cherries. Brilliant, right? But then the D train broke down, so I had to get out of the subway and call an Uber. The driver was so fascinating —"

"Thank you for doing that, sweetie," Maggie said docilely. "Now would you mind terribly mixing the Manhattans? We're all dying."

Edie, Celia, and Ollie roped the unsuspecting Hugo into playing horsey. They always did that with the new guy; I remembered them riding on Josh's back around the loft a few years ago. I was afraid it would be weird to be here with Josh and Hugo together, but it wasn't, not really. I had gotten to the point, I realized, where it felt more normal not being with Josh than being with him. I was surprised to find myself able to watch him and Kelsey chatting happily together without feeling any jealousy. I prodded my psychic tooth with my figurative tongue. Nope, nothing.

Hugo, though. I couldn't help thinking that he looked so fine lying there on the floor as the kids tied him up. He was gorgeous, yes, but as Stella said, he was also so sweet, so sensitive, which made him seem even more masculine.

I felt Maggie's hand on my arm. She was carrying a salad bowl to the table.

"So," she said. "Really?"

"Not really."

"What are you waiting for?"

We were all trying to stuff one more of the

delicious ravioli in our mouths when Frankie said, "So what do you do, Hugo?"

"I'm an actor," said Hugo.

Frankie laughed. "I'm a teacher, so we don't have that in common, though we may be the two worst-paid people here."

"Do you think so?" said Maggie.

"Well, I know Kelsey's gone Hollywood, so she's mega rich," said Frankie. "Josh sold his company last year and bought a new one, so he's doing okay. And Maggie is an overnight sensation after working for thirty years."

We all raised our glasses to Maggie.

"Of course, there's Liza," Frankie continued. "She might be the poorest of us all, but that could change if her show's a hit."

"Is that so?" said Hugo. "Excuse me, but where is the . . ."

Maggie directed Hugo to the bathroom, and as soon as he was out of the room, everyone leaned across the table to me.

"What the fuck are you doing here with Hugo Fielding?" Kelsey said.

"Hugo Fielding?" said Frankie.

"Yes," said Kelsey.

"Hugo Fielding the movie star?"

"Yes," I said.

"God, I'm an idiot," said Frankie.

Maggie patted their shoulder and kissed

them on the cheek. "That's okay, sweet-heart. You still had those cherries on your mind."

Kelsey's cupcake catastrophe meant that for dessert we were reduced to eating whatever ice cream we could find in Maggie's freezer, which, thanks to Frankie's sweet tooth, was a lot. Advanced scrounging yielded nine half-eaten cartons, which meant we each got our own carton and then some. The kids were thrilled, and ran off with their individual cartons and spoons to watch *Paw Patrol.*

We stayed at the table until the cartons were empty and it was dark outside, candles burning low, the dregs of Frankie's delicious Manhattans sticky in the bottom of the crystal pitcher. There was something about the night, the candlelight, the warm faces around the table that invited cosmic conversation.

"What would you do," Maggie said to the group, "if you could do anything you wanted right now?"

"Well, obviously, I'd do something that paid far more money," Frankie said. "I could go into labor organizing, perhaps, or write pastoral poetry."

"I'm just holding my breath that I get to keep all the great things that have come into my life — this wonderful person" — Maggie took Frankie's hand — "my daughters and stepson, my career."

"If I could wave a magic wand," Kelsey said, "I'd have my person and my baby and move career down to third on my list."

"I'm kind of feeling the same way," said Josh. "It's scary getting up into your thirties never having been married or having children."

"Oh, it's not so bad," said Hugo.

"You might be the most famous eternal bachelor in the world," said Maggie. "Why did you never settle down?"

Kelsey smirked. "Why would he?"

"No, I'd like to have met the right person and to have fallen in love forever," said Hugo. "I'd love to have the cozy marriage, the three kids, the mountain of shoes by the door."

We couldn't help it, we all looked at the mountain of shoes near Maggie's door.

"I always thought it would happen," Hugo continued, "but then when I passed forty-five, I decided my time was up."

"Your time isn't up," Kelsey said, almost angrily. "You can have a kid when you're seventy if you want."

"But I don't want to," said Hugo.

260

"So what do you want?" I said, unable to resist.

"I want this," said Hugo. "A big pasta dinner every night, with ice cream for dessert. If I could do whatever I wanted, I'd never take another CrossFit class in my life. I'd get old and fat and happy and know I was loved and wanted anyway."

That brought the discussion to a standstill as we all, for one sweet moment, felt like our lives were better than his.

Finally, Josh broke the silence. "So, Liza," he said. "You haven't said what you'd want, if you could have anything."

I thought of the list I'd made when I left the island more than four months ago. What had been on it?

Home. Still wanted one, still didn't have one.

Job, ditto.

Money. Had a little, not enough.

I could say now that the baby was healthy, thank God.

Friends. I loved being back together with my friends instead of marooned with my memories.

I hadn't put love or a man or a relationship on my list last time, but did I want that now? I'd been a firm *no* for so long. But Hugo had finally nudged me over the edge to *maybe.*

"Liza?" said Maggie.

It had been five years since I'd stood in this room and transformed myself into a younger woman and started a new life. I'd lived as that person for three years and then I'd thought about and written about and talked about that time for two more years. And I was done. Not as in vowing to quit. Done as in feeling the wind change like it does in *The Wizard of Oz,* and you know it's blowing you somewhere new.

"I want to start over," I said.

"As long as you do it in New York," said Maggie.

"Don't change too much," said Josh.

"We just don't want you to start over without us," said Hugo.

While everyone milled around at the door embracing and chatting — the Italian good-bye, Maggie called it — Kelsey pulled me aside.

"Remember that thing you said, about how we were never allowed to date each other's ex-boyfriends?" she said.

"That was your thing," I said. "Not mine."

She frowned. "I thought it was your thing. Anyway, Josh and I have been hanging out. . . ."

Kelsey and Josh. Josh and Kelsey. It made so much sense. Did I have a pang of jealousy? A moment of weirdness? I'd be lying if I said no. But I also sincerely thought it was a great match for both of them.

"You have my blessing," I said.

"Really?" She jumped up and down and clapped her hands.

"What about Hugo?" I said. "Do I have your blessing about that?"

"It's not about me," she said. "It's about him and Stella."

"I really don't think that's happening," I said.

She made a skeptical face. "I'm pretty sure it is."

"I'm pretty sure it's not," I said. "In any case, I'm a big girl. I just don't want to screw things up between you and me."

"Okay," she said somberly. "If you're really set on ignoring every piece of advice I've ever given you, go ahead."

Hugo and I rode down silently in the elevator with Kelsey and Josh.

"I'm heading downtown," Josh said.

"I'm going that way too," said Kelsey.

I began walking backward. "Okay, see you later!" I said, waving.

Hugo began walking backward beside me.

"We don't have to do this all the way

home, do we?" he said.

I liked the sound of "we" and "home" in the same sentence, though I wasn't really sure what that meant. We were going together to the one block that separated our buildings, and then we'd figure it out.

I knew he wanted to be with me; I could feel it. And I wanted it too. Of course I did. He was a wonderful guy, warm and funny and smart and handsome and sweet and sexy and tall. I loved him. I just *loved* him.

I really had never felt like this. It was like the two halves of the picture came together, and the person I was wildly attracted to was also a person I loved being with. A person who respected my work. A person who was good to me.

But how was it possible that such an amazing person could want me? How could somebody who could have *anybody* want *me*? I wasn't being falsely modest. I didn't have a big self-image problem. Yes, I thought I was nice-looking and in decent shape for my age, and I was confident that I was smart and thoughtful. I laughed easily, and people — men and women — usually liked me. I was a pretty good catch, for a hipster entrepreneur in Brooklyn or a dentist in New Jersey. Not for a world-famous movie star. If I went out with Hugo, would I ever really trust him? Would I ever stop questioning whether I was good enough?

"Are you and Stella having an affair?" I said.

He let out a bark of laughter. "You asked me that before and I told you no. Why are you asking me again?"

"Something doesn't feel right," I said.

It was subtle; the kind of thing that, when I was younger, I discounted and pushed out of the way. It was the same kind of discomfort I was feeling when I walked down the aisle to marry David, for instance. Not listening to it had probably helped me push through some fear in a positive way, but it also had gotten me into some bad situations that were even more difficult to untangle.

"I swear to you, I am not having an affair with Stella," he said.

But what he said was the opposite of reassuring.

"I haven't heard that since the night of the mushrooms," I said. "That phony voice."

"I am not having an affair with Stella," he said in his deep, sober, pharmaceutical-commercial voice.

I laughed, despite myself.

"You swear to me that you and Stella are not together."

"I swear."

"What is real?" I said.

"You are real; I am real," he said. "The way I feel about you is real."

He reached over and took my hand. We were walking down the street that separated our two buildings. I could go left with him, back to his place, or turn right and go to mine. I was on the brink of turning left when I saw her, standing outside his building. It was a warm night, but she was shivering. She was also smoking and pacing back and forth in her bare feet. She had, it was clear as we got closer, been crying for quite some time.

"Where have you been?" she shouted.

"What's happened?" he said to her. "What's going on?"

"I need to talk to you," she said.

He broke apart from me and went to her.

"Come on," he said in a soothing voice. I noticed him put a steady hand on her back. "Let's go inside."

"I don't need to go inside!" she screamed. "I can say everything I need to say right here."

"You don't want to do that," he said, his tone calm and even. "Come on, now. Let's go upstairs."

Stella took a big last drag on her cigarette and dropped the butt to the pavement, where it smoldered dangerously close to her bare toes. Then she blew the smoke in my direction.

I wasn't sure what to do. When Hugo said, *Let's go upstairs,* did he mean me too? I took one baby step in their direction.

"Not *you*," Stella said.

That was real. She was real. Realer than all the pretty words Hugo had been feeding me, or all the lies I'd been telling myself.

# TWENTY-ONE

When Caitlin asked if we could take the Volvo for a drive so she could show me something, I thought we were headed for some far-flung neighborhood in Brooklyn or Queens — Red Hook or Breezy Point — to see a house she and Ravi wanted to buy. Then, when she drove through the Holland Tunnel into New Jersey, I figured we were going to Hoboken or maybe Jersey City. And was astonished when she kept going, all the way to Homewood.

"Did you buy a house in Homewood?" I asked my daughter, amazed.

But she only shook her head no, smiling mysteriously.

After spending the past months in big-city Los Angeles and New York, Homewood looked different to me: smaller and pokier, but also more beautiful. It was hard to believe that this leafy village with big, comfy-looking family houses was twelve miles outside New York.

"There's the playground where we used to smoke pot in middle school," Caitlin said.

"You smoked pot in middle school?"

"Duh, Mom."

Caitlin had seemed like a little girl in middle school, at least in the first half of it. She wore purple tee shirts and flowered overalls and bows in her hair. Her best friend had been Amanda Posner; in sixth grade, they still played Barbies together, though I knew they had a mutual pact of secrecy. Now I understood that Barbie wasn't the only thing they'd kept secret.

"I smoked pot in LA," I said. "Well, edibles mostly. And one night I did mushrooms."

"Mom!" Caitlin sounded a lot more outraged than I had at her confession. "I hope you're not doing that kind of thing now."

"Of course not," I said. "Pot is legal there."

Though if it was legal in New York, I would totally be doing it. And the mushrooms were strictly a one-time thing.

"You can't do that around the baby," Caitlin said.

"I know that," I told her.

Eloise was almost ready to leave the hospital. She might not have been quite smiling or focusing yet, but she was spend-

269

ing several hours a day in a regular bassinet, even nursing rather than feeding through a tube, which understandably thrilled Caitlin. Caitlin and Ravi were more relaxed and excited now that their daughter was clearly okay and would soon be coming home.

Homewood held memories for me on almost every block, in every shop and restaurant and landmark. There was the corner where we waited for the school bus when Caitlin was in kindergarten, the coffee shop where I had Friday lunches with my moms group, the post office where someone got shot, the pond where we'd all ice-skated that winter when everything stayed frozen through March.

Most of the memories were good, but it was still too much: I felt assaulted at every turn, so filled up with the past that I lost all sense of who I was now.

Caitlin pulled up outside a three-story dark-blue house with a wraparound porch. Her childhood best friend Amanda Posner's house.

"Are we going to see Amanda?" I said brightly.

I had always liked Amanda, and I remembered her mom, a librarian, as being smart and sweet. I always loved talking books with her.

"Amanda moved to the Bay Area to work for Facebook," Caitlin said.

Actually, that rang a dim bell.

"She's pregnant, and her parents are moving to San Francisco to be near her," Caitlin told me. "We're renting their house."

Once she said it, it made perfect sense, but I had not seen it coming.

Caitlin already had the key in her hand and led me down the front path to the welcoming front porch, where the wicker furniture I remembered from the girls' childhood was still arrayed.

"They're leaving a lot of their furniture — isn't that great?" Caitlin said. "And they gave us a real deal on the rent. They're not ready to sell yet — they want to see whether Amanda and her wife really stay in the Bay Area — but if they do, they'll give us an insider's price. And this way we get to try out suburban life without making a major commitment. Isn't it amazing?"

It *was* amazing, I agreed once we got inside: so much space for the money, on a quiet street with plenty of charm, and enough furniture to fill up the corners until Caitlin and Ravi figured out what they were going to do long-term. I was glad she'd decided to leave the city and take this practical step. It was so hard, once you had a baby, to give up the idea that you were no longer cool, living the sophisticated urban life, when the fact was you were spending all your nights at home getting the baby to sleep and then collapsing yourself.

"It's walking distance to our old house!" Caitlin pointed out.

I wasn't sure what the significance of that was, but that was one place in Homewood I had no desire to visit. Too many ghosts, too much heartache at the way it all had ended.

Caitlin showed me around the four bedrooms on the second floor, including a nursery painted a beautiful shade of periwinkle blue. There were two bathrooms with pretty antique tile.

"Ravi and I can't believe how big this place is," she said delightedly. "We're going to have to call each other on the phone when we want to talk."

I remember having that same feeling myself when we first moved to Homewood. I loved living in a place I felt my already growing life could keep growing into, a place so capacious that the only limits were the ones I set myself.

"And now for the best of all," Caitlin said, her eyes twinkling.

She led me up a flight of steep blue-painted stairs to the third floor, a typical feature in Homewood houses, most of which had been built around the turn of the last century. These top floors, with gables and pitched ceilings, had been servants' quarters before the First World War and had morphed over time into teenager lairs, home offices, and nanny apartments.

This third floor had three rooms, wide-plank wooden floors painted the same blue as the stairs, a bathroom, and a tiny kitchenette along one wall.

"You can have a live-in nanny!" I said.

A cloud darkened Caitlin's face.

"I thought *you'd* live here," she said.

*"Me?"* I was astonished. And appalled.

"This place is big enough that we can all have our own space," Caitlin explained. "And once you're done shooting the pilot, you're going to need a place to live."

"I really appreciate the offer, Caitlin," I said. "But I don't want to live in Homewood again."

"I don't get it," she said. "How many times did you tell me I should move to Homewood?"

"And you told me you would never move to New Jersey!"

"But then it turned out you were right; this does make more sense!" Caitlin cried. "And now I got offered a promotion at

273

work, but if I want it I have to start Monday, and that's the day after they're sending Eloise home from the hospital."

I thought she was going to have a panic attack right there before me.

"All right, let's think about this," I said. I steered her over to a comfy pink-flowered chair near the window. "I know there's a nanny service —"

"Mom, Eloise was a preemie! She's been living in the hospital for six weeks! This will be her first time home and I've got to turn around and leave her every day!"

Caitlin broke down weeping then. She seemed absolutely heartbroken.

"Honey, maybe you're not ready to go back to work," I said, my hand on her shoulder. "Maybe after all you've been through, you might want to take this time and stay home with the baby."

"Mom, I can't do that, we need the money!" she burst out.

She got up and started bustling around the attic room. I'd forgotten this: When she was a teenager having regular temper tantrums, directed at us or at a boy or a friend or a teacher, she'd rant and clean at the same time, unaware she was doing it. There was always a consolation prize when we fought: Her room would be spotless.

Now she was rearranging the books on the bookshelf by color and size, moving methodically left to right, not looking at me. It was disconcerting, but she'd probably say more and say it more honestly if she was moving while we talked.

"I thought Ravi's residency was over," I said. "Isn't he going to get a job?"

"He got that fellowship!" she said. "They pick only like one in ten thousand people. He can't turn it down."

I was trying to think of another alternative that wasn't me, but I wasn't getting far. She'd rejected the idea of a nanny, so she would definitely not be up for day care. I mulled she and Ravi both going part-time, but given her promotion and his prestigious new fellowship, they were bound to be working more not less.

"You said you would help me," my daughter said.

"I also told you I couldn't be your full-time caregiver."

Caitlin paused for a moment before she spoke again. "Mom, you know when I was a little girl and I used to tell you that you were the best mommy in the whole wide world?" she said. "I really meant it, and even when I got older and realized it was the kind of thing most kids said, I still thought it was

275

true. I think it's true now. You were always so warm and loving and creative and *fun*. I can't think of anyone else I'd rather have taking care of my little girl."

I was misting up by this point. "Not even you?" I said gently.

"Mom, if it was practical for me to stay home with her, I'd do that, but it's not and it's breaking my heart. If I'm going to go back to work and hold it all together, I need to know you're here with her." She stopped for a second and then hastened to add, "Not forever. But for now."

The room had four corners, and I felt as if I were backed into at least three of them. I loved my granddaughter. I loved my daughter. I kind of theoretically loved my son-in-law. But I really really really, deep down in my soul, did not want to stay home with a baby. And that made me a terrible person.

"I might want to write another book," I said.

"Didn't you always say you wished you'd written when I was a baby?" Caitlin said. "That you wished you'd been able to figure out how to do both?"

"Yeah, but that doesn't mean I did figure it out."

"Mom, if I had another plan I'd take it,

but this whole time you've been telling me over and over that you want to be here for me and help me with the baby . . . well, this is it. I need your help." Her tears had dried now; her mouth was set in a hard line. "Are you going to help me or not?"

I wanted to say no, but not as much as I didn't want to say no. What were the big things I wanted to do instead anyway? Write some fake story that nobody wanted to publish? Live in Maggie's closet, pining for my secret movie-star love? It was ridiculous, adolescent, and what did any of it matter? Was I really not mature enough to tuck away my insignificant personal desires for a while and help my daughter get her career and her family on its feet?

I was finally leaving my younger life behind — I could see that version of me fading into the distance — but I had nothing to replace it. It was time to put away all my childish fantasies and get real: There was nothing I could do or even dream of doing that was more important than this.

I grabbed Kelsey at the first coffee break. I couldn't hang around the set thinking only about having to tell her.

"I told Caitlin I'd move to New Jersey and take care of her baby," I blurted.

"Wow," Kelsey said. She was eating a Krispy Kreme donut, an unusual occurrence for her. "Wanna trade places?"

That was not the response I'd expected.

"Uh, kind of?" I said.

"Oh, come on, you don't want to be here from morning to night dealing with Madame Stella and her Romeo," said Kelsey. "We should have been finished shooting this pilot two weeks ago, but somehow Stella keeps finding ways to drag things out."

"Can't you get her back on schedule?"

"She's paying the bills," Kelsey said. "I think this is all an elaborate justification for extending her time in New York."

"I'm not sure you want to be alone in the suburbs with an infant," I said to Kelsey.

"Are you going to do anything besides take care of the baby?" Kelsey asked me.

"I actually have a new novel idea," I told her. "It's called *The Matriarch.*"

Kelsey laughed. "Now you're writing about your new life."

Incredibly enough, that hadn't occurred to me until she said it.

"What about *your* new life," I said. "How are things with Josh?"

She shrugged and looked away, but she was smiling. "We'll see," she said.

"We'll see . . . . whether you two keep going out? What develops between you?"

"All of the above," she said. "I love Josh, you know that. I'm just not sure yet whether I can *love* Josh."

I didn't know if it would be helpful or otherwise to state what was obvious to me, but it went to the heart of why I thought they'd be so perfect for each other.

"You both want kids," I said. "I was hoping maybe you'd found your baby daddy."

Kelsey shrugged. "We'll see," she said. "I've actually been thinking that maybe if Josh and I don't work out, I'll have a kid on my own."

"Really? What changed your mind?"

"Maybe being in New York? I can imagine having a different kind of career here that might make it possible."

"We can get together for play dates," I told her, half teasing.

"Maybe we could start a moms group," she said. "I know someone else who could join."

"Who?" I said.

Right at that moment, Stella walked by the cafeteria door, talking a mile a minute to Hugo. Kelsey jutted her chin in their direction.

It took me a moment to catch on. And then I literally lost my breath. "What?" I said. "You're kidding."

"There hasn't been any announcement," she said, "but the wardrobe mistress came to me and said Stella was popping out of all the clothes we bought for her. In all the places that indicate a pregnancy."

"And the baby is Hugo's?" I said, though I didn't find that so hard to believe, especially after the other night. In fact, it explained a lot about Stella's behavior, and his.

"She's already said she doesn't have sex with Barry," Kelsey said. "Who else's would it be?"

I was suddenly glad I had a solid reason for quitting the show so I didn't have to watch this romance unfold for another minute.

"I guess you were right about him," I said. "Would it be okay if I slipped away this morning? I'm not really doing anything essential."

"You're always doing something essential," Kelsey said. "You're keeping me sane."

"Call and text me anytime you want," I said. "But I know you're going to be fine."

Out of the corner of my eye, I spotted Hugo heading in our direction. I did not want to get caught having to explain anything to him. Fool me once and all that.

Without even taking the time to say a proper goodbye to poor Kelsey, I hopped up, blew her a little kiss, and hurried away. I might have heard Hugo calling my name as I walked off the set, but I pretended I didn't.

## TWENTY-TWO

I bounce-walked, my wailing granddaughter strapped to my chest, the length of the kitchen. Then I turned around and bounce-walked back. I was singing "Rock-a-Bye Baby," alternating with "Hound Dog." They seemed to be the only songs I knew, but maybe that was because I was exhausted and my brain was on autopilot.

I'd been taking care of Eloise for three days now, and every time I thought I was establishing a modicum of the beginning of a routine, everything changed. She cried in the morning, she cried at night. She slept and then ate, or she ate and then slept. Or none of the above.

Finally, her cries downshifted to whimpers. I kept bounce-walking, switching from crooning Elvis to acting as a human white-noise machine. *"Sssssssh,"* I soothed. *"Sssssssssssh."*

I felt my phone vibrate in my back pocket.

I'd learned quickly to turn off the text chime: Eloise seemed able to detect the sound from a hundred feet away. I slipped the phone out now and read the text from Kelsey as I bounced and shushed: a photo of Hugo comforting a crying Stella, which Kelsey had captioned with an emoji of a cat with its head exploding.

*Lol,* I typed, and pressed send. I had to say, I was getting pretty good at working my phone while caring for the baby, essential given that it was my only connection to the world beyond diapers and bottles.

I felt Eloise soften and grow warmer against my chest as she dropped off to sleep, her breath rhythmic and audible. She smelled delicious. I kept bounce-walking, kept *sssssssh*-ing, climbing the stairs until we were upstairs in the nursery. Slowly, quietly, I unzipped the carrier. Gently, steadily, I lifted her out. I lowered her toward the crib, set her on the mattress, slid my hands out from beneath her.

She started screaming again.

I gave myself a moment to fall back flat on the floor, staring at the ceiling and building the will to cope. Then I lifted her back into the carrier, which I might as well have hot-glued to my shirt, bouncing harder this time, singing faster. When she finally fell asleep once again, twenty minutes later, I knew better than to attempt to put her in the crib. Instead, I lowered myself onto the couch, thinking that I could write by hand while she slept against me. If I could manage not to fall asleep myself.

My plan was to make some notes for *The Matriarch.* Maybe this was ideal, writing about some fantasy version of my post-fifty life while I was living the real version. I could jot some notes on characters and settings for *The Matriarch* around the edges of caring for Eloise. The matriarch herself, for instance, is extremely rich, having built a business in something practical, like construction or luxury car sales. The matriarch presides over a complement of children and children-in-law along with grandchildren, though she does so from a distance, and often in the arms of her exotic secret lover.

That was good. I should write that down. Except I didn't have a pen. I struggled back to my feet, the slumbering baby warm and heavy against me, found a pen, sat back down, and opened the notebook.

*Matriarch,* I wrote at the top of the page. Then underlined it twice. I had a strong sense of déjà vu. I'd done exactly this, I remembered. Right before I left Maine, when I was thinking about what I wanted to do and to have before I turned fifty. None of which I'd done or had.

I wanted to start creating the characters for *The Matriarch,* but I couldn't stop thinking of Kelsey's text. Why was Stella crying? What was up with her and Hugo? I knew Stella was a mad Instagrammer, so with my newly dexterous thumbs I found her Instagram profile. No mascara-streaked tears on that page, only Stella's toe cleavage showing off her new red snakeskin pumps, a selfie of her wearing a full-body black leotard that seemed to reveal a baby bump, and a close-up of what I recognized as the side of Hugo's face: rough beard and tender cheek.

Blech. I shut down the phone and tossed it to the other end of the couch. If I had any time at all, I needed to spend it writing. Or resting. Or fighting back the tide of diapers and bottles and tiny little clothes that needed washing.

Except I wasn't going to do any of that, because the baby started fussing again. I stood up, taking the notebook and pen and, okay, the phone with me. Could I write as I walked? Not possible. Maybe if I stood at the kitchen counter, bouncing and swaying as I wrote, I could get something done.

But there was nowhere to put the notebook down on the kitchen counter, because every surface was covered with dirty bottles and empty containers that had contained Caitlin's frozen breast milk, along with my mug full of now-cold coffee and everybody's breakfast dishes, a pile of diapers, a spit-up-covered onesie, and cereal boxes and a box of wipes and newspapers from the last few days.

I couldn't focus at all in this chaos, so I moved around quickly straightening up, the baby still strapped against me. The faster I moved, the quieter she grew, although the second I stopped moving, she began fussing again.

It was a beautiful day outside. Maybe since I couldn't write now, I should take her for a walk. We could both get some air, which would undoubtedly be good for our health and our moods.

Homewood really was a beautiful town. I'd forgotten how beautiful, or maybe I'd just blocked it. It was painful being back in the place I loved but that had been lost to me, like being at a party with an ex you'd never gotten over. An ex who didn't even notice you were there.

It did feel good to breathe fresh air, though, and to move beyond the four walls of that house. Eloise snuggled against me, I snapped a photo of her and posted it to

Caitlin and Ravi's photo sharing app. Within seconds, both had liked the photo and Caitlin had commented: *Angel.*

Walking down the street in Homewood, everything was oddly the same, but different. The same pink hydrangea bush was blooming in front of the dark green house, except the old hedges had been torn out. Some of the houses were painted different colors. There were new cars in the driveways, a tree had been cut down, or a different dog barked behind a freshly painted fence. And all the people were different. School had started for the year, and kids climbed off buses or walked home in pairs or gangs; so many children that I could almost imagine they were the neighbor kids and classmates of Caitlin's I'd known: freckled Robin and rascal-y Miles and somber Elizabeth, who had once told me her mother slept all day and left her all alone.

"That's not going to happen to you," I said aloud to Eloise, cradling her rump. She was, of course, fast asleep.

Another text came in. Maggie this time, saying only *How u?*

*OK,* I typed back. *U?*

She sent a picture of a British Airways plane on the tarmac. *Off to London!* she

287

wrote. *C u soon.* And then some hearts.

"I want to be you," I said aloud, though I only texted back more hearts. I needed to stop looking at my phone. I had thought, before I went out, that I wouldn't walk up our old street, but now I was in such a bad mood I figured it couldn't make me feel any worse. I'd managed to avoid that ever since we moved away, even when I came back to visit friends. It hurt too much to be an outsider looking at the house I'd cleaned and painted and renovated, the house where I'd brought my daughter home from the hospital and made love with my husband and took care of my parents before they died.

I felt like a ghost drawn inexorably to my old home. Walking slowly up the street, with one of the baby's feet held lightly in each hand, I expected that any moment one of my former neighbors would come outside and recognize me. We'd talk and I'd tell them what I was doing and say yes, I was living here with Caitlin now, helping with the baby. Maybe we'd make plans to have coffee or they'd invite me over for dinner. Maybe I'd rediscover some wonderful element of my life I'd forgotten but that had been here waiting for me all this time.

But the children who raced through the

yards were not children I knew. All the kids who'd lived on the block when we'd lived there had grown up now and moved away, or maybe moved around the corner and were raising kids of their own. Every time a door opened or a car pulled in a driveway, I expected to see someone I knew, half dreading and half craving the connection. But it might as well have been a hundred years and not five since I'd lived here.

I stopped across the street from my old house, still swaying to keep the baby asleep, trying to catch a glimpse in a window or find some clue that would tell me something about the life that was unfolding there now. They'd painted the place, a boring gray I never would have chosen. There was a red tricycle on the front lawn.

I took a photo, feeling like a spy, and texted it to Caitlin. A second later the front door opened and a young woman walked out onto the porch, holding a toddler by the hand. She was blond, the child was a boy. I'd never met the people who'd bought the house from me. It was too painful to go to the closing, so the lawyer handled it, and I couldn't remember their names. This might be her; she might remember who I was.

I imagined walking across the street,

introducing myself, asking if I could have a look around inside, revisiting the house I'd loved so well. And then, what, say goodbye again? I wasn't sure I could bear that.

The woman put the toddler on the tricycle and pushed him into the driveway, where he was able to pedal by himself. She looked over at me. I smiled and raised my hand in greeting. She raised her hand back but looked more puzzled than friendly. Then she turned her back on me and followed the toddler down the driveway toward the backyard.

"Bye," I said softly.

My phone vibrated in my pocket with another text. I expected it to be Caitlin, responding to the image of the house. But instead it was Hugo.

*Where are you?* he wrote.

I thought of all the ways I might respond.

Then my phone started ringing. I jumped and hurried to turn it off. I wished I could throw it into the bushes. Eloise shifted in the carrier and whimpered, and, rubbing her little back, I took off again at a faster clip, back to my daughter's home.

I kept trying to find ways to get some writing done around caring for the baby. After all, she slept many hours a day, if only in

290

short spurts or in the carrier. I'd swear that the minute she dropped off, I was going to sit down and write no matter if there were dirty diapers on the floor or ten texts from Kelsey on my phone. Or write while I stood up and swayed. Or write while I danced. Or write in my head and put it on paper later, as if I had any hope of remembering anything once the baby finally dropped off to sleep, when all I wanted to do was pass out myself.

It wasn't that a week was so very long to take care of a baby without writing. Eloise was so tiny, her system so undeveloped, that I knew she would fall into a more predictable routine in a few months. And I was new at this too, out of practice. I'd figure it out with a little time.

That's what I'd told myself back when Caitlin was born too. Those days were flooding back over me as if the twenty-six intervening years had never happened. Eloise looked so much like baby Caitlin that gazing into her eyes sometimes made me feel as if I were time traveling, not only in terms of what I was doing but of who I was inside.

In those moments I felt exactly as I'd felt as a brand-new mother, a dizzying mix of infatuation, boredom, tenderness, frustration, terror, love. And a nightmarish sense of disappearing as my identity merged with the baby's.

I'd chided myself all these years for not being that mythical writer mom who types away in the minivan while waiting for preschool to let out, for soccer practice to be over. If I'd wanted it badly enough, if I were more talented, if I was really meant to be a writer, I would have managed to make it work.

Now it took only a week at home with Eloise to understand that it was impossible. Virtually impossible. As impossible as me becoming a senator, say, or an Olympic athlete. Sure, everybody wanted to be that mom who rocks the cradle with one hand while writing bestsellers with the other, and yet so few made it. And why was that? Because it very nearly could not be done.

My mom friend Joanne used to say that staying home with kids was like giving yourself up to Jesus or I guess any kind of messiah. You couldn't hold back, you couldn't do it halfway. You had to devote your whole life to your god, aka the baby.

If you wanted to take care of your family and your home, then you had a full-time job. And if you also wanted to do something creative or go back to school or start a business, then you had another full-time job and needed someone else to take care of your kids.

I'd always said I loved being a full-time mom, but now I couldn't help wondering, had I really loved all those endless years made up of endless days devoted to one small person with extremely persistent needs? Or had I been bored and trapped and just ashamed to say so? Or bored and trapped but afraid there was nothing better out there for me. Or maybe I'd chosen to spend those years with my child, however stultifying, because I realized the only alternative was not having enough time with her at all.

It seemed to be a miracle that Eloise was asleep, in her actual crib, when Mrs. Whitney's assistant, Betty, called. It was the end of the first week, on Friday afternoon, and I was attempting to cycle through a load of wash. They liked to do things the old-fashioned way at Empirical Press, preferring a visit to a call, a call to an email, an email to a — well, that was as informal as they got.

"Hello, dear," Betty said. Betty always acted like not quite a mother, more like the college resident advisor responsible for your welfare. "How is everything going with you?"

I told Betty I'd been taking care of my granddaughter and so hadn't been working on the show or doing any writing. I figured that she was calling to tell me she had a tax form I had to sign or as a prelude to a conversation with Mrs. Whitney. I was managing expectations, all expectations.

"Mrs. Whitney asked me to call you, dear, to let you know that she's in the hospital and to ask a favor of you."

"Oh no," I said. "What's going on?"

"Everything's fine," Betty assured me. "She's just in for some tests. But there are some papers she needs you to bring her."

"She needs *me* to bring her?" I said.

"Yes, dear. She didn't give me any details other than to get in touch with you and ask if you could pick up an envelope at the office and deliver it to her by hand."

"Where is she?" I asked.

Because of course I was going to bring Mrs. Whitney the documents, whatever they were and no matter why she needed them. Maybe an addendum to the book contract we both needed to sign, or sales figures she wanted to go over with me? And what kind of tests demanded that Mrs. Whitney stay at the hospital anyway?

All Betty would tell me was the name of the hospital, and she said she'd leave the envelope with the lobby attendant at Empirical's building. I promised her I'd get the envelope and go to see Mrs. Whitney before the weekend was over.

When Caitlin got home from work that night, I wanted to talk to her right away about arranging my visit to Mrs. Whitney. The more I thought about it, the more worried I was, and the more urgent it seemed that I get there as soon as possible. Although Eloise was fussing when Caitlin got home, I said there was something I needed to discuss. But Caitlin held up her hand to stop me.

"Just let me wash my hands and get these clothes off," she said. She disappeared upstairs.

Caitlin was exhausted. She was waking up in the middle of the night to nurse, then working a long day learning a new job. She did not want to leave early or ask her supervisor for any concessions, afraid she'd lose the job she'd worked so hard to get. And the commute to and from the city was adding an extra hour and a half to her day that she had not bargained for when she decided to go after the job. The situation was difficult, for all of us.

Eloise was fussing, as she usually was in the evening. I circled the living room, rocking her until her mother came down fifteen minutes later in leggings and a big shirt.

"Is there any dinner?" Caitlin asked.

I knew that if I were a really good caregiver and housekeeper, I would have dinner on the table. But I could barely manage to call for takeout.

"There's pasta," I said. "Or frozen Indian."

Caitlin sighed heavily.

"I'm sorry," I said. "I know you've had a long day."

"It was the commute from hell," she said. "And I'm starving."

"I can pull some dinner together," I said, "if you take over with Eloise."

She eyed the baby warily. Her crying had grown louder.

"I'm so tired," she said.

"Go sit down," I suggested. "I'll call Mr. Dino's and order a pie."

Our emergency dinner supplier for more than twenty-five years.

I could tell Caitlin was too exhausted and distracted to listen if I brought up my trip into the city to see Mrs. Whitney, so we turned on an *Office* rerun and took turns holding the baby and eating pizza. When

Eloise fell asleep, we both collapsed.

When I came downstairs in the morning, I was surprised to find Caitlin already up, alone and working at the kitchen table as sunlight streamed in through the window.

"Did Ravi take Eloise out?" I asked, growing hopeful.

"No, she's asleep, believe it or not," Caitlin said. "She went down after her early morning feed, so I figured I'd get to work on this report that's due Monday."

This was good news.

"I have to go into the city to see Mrs. Whitney," I said. "Maybe I should go right now."

I'd quickly learned to be fully dressed the minute I hopped out of bed, or I might not get any chance at all. And I wanted to be ready to undertake my errand to see Mrs. Whitney as soon as I got the opportunity.

"Can't it wait a bit?" she said. "She's been down for two hours and I'm afraid she's going to wake up again before I finish this."

I could wait. Mrs. Whitney wasn't expecting me at any certain time. She wasn't expecting me this morning at all. Caitlin was under a lot of pressure at work. She needed to work at night and on weekends to catch up.

I didn't want to seem unsupportive, knowing how sensitive Caitlin was to my position on her working motherhood. I was truly proud of her. I appreciated how much stress she must be under. But something was niggling at me.

"Can't Ravi take over while you do the report?"

"He's playing basketball," Caitlin said.

Ravi deserved to relax, of course he did. He'd worked so late every night this week that he never made it home for Eloise's bedtime.

But I had been there for every bedtime this week, often alone. I was about to visit my longtime publisher and boss, with whom I was close, in the hospital. And I had a mysterious errand that needed to be performed as soon as possible.

"I'm sorry," I made myself say. "But I really need to go. Can I have the car keys?"

My old Volvo was still the household's only car.

"Ravi took the car," said Caitlin.

"I've got to run, then," I said, heading for the door, "so I can catch the 9:10 train."

I didn't feel guilty about leaving Caitlin and Ravi to deal with the baby on their own, or about taking time away from my baby granddaughter. I only felt guilty about how happy I was to be doing it.

# TWENTY-THREE

It was a shock to see Mrs. Whitney lying there in the hospital bed, dressed in a printed gown rather than a Chanel jacket, her lips pale, her earlobes unadorned, no little dog in his Gucci case at her side.

"Darling!" she cried, nonplussed. She ran her hand over her white hair and pulled her hospital gown up at the neck. "Betty didn't tell me you were coming this morning."

"I've been taking care of my baby grand-daughter," I said. "I wasn't sure when I would be able to get away."

"It's awfully good of you to take the time to visit me," she said.

I didn't want to pry — my relationship with Mrs. Whitney was always more profes-sionally buttoned-up than personally reveal-ing — but I couldn't very well pretend we were meeting at the Century Club. And what kind of tests required an in-hospital stay? As I'd just witnessed when Caitlin gave birth, they usually kicked you out of the place ASAP.

"What's going on?" I said. "Betty said something about tests?"

Mrs. Whitney waved her hand dismissively. "It's so ridiculous, poking here and there, trying to find something wrong. I keep telling the doctor that at my age, if you start looking for a problem, you're going to find one."

"But . . . there must have been something that made you go to the doctor in the first place," I said delicately.

"Oh God, no, I loathe the doctor. But you know, Betty schedules the checkups every year, and then she watches like a hawk to make sure I go. And of course they do the standard blood tests and one thing's high and the other thing is low. I just want them to make their little diagnosis so I can go home."

"Okay," I said, not entirely sure whether I believed her. Then I remembered the mysterious envelope, which had been weighing heavily on me since Betty first mentioned it. I extracted it from my purse and handed it to her.

"What's in here that only I can bring you?" I asked, trying to sound mildly curious rather than desperately anxious.

300

"We'll talk about that in a bit," Mrs. Whitney said. She tucked the envelope under her blanket. "But first tell me, how is the television show going?"

"I'm not really involved anymore, since I started watching my granddaughter, so I'm not sure how it's going," I said carefully. "I know Stella has been difficult."

I got texts from Kelsey every day, detailing Stella's sometimes hilarious, sometimes outrageous, sometimes obstreperous behavior.

"I thought it was going so beautifully," Mrs. Whitney said.

I hated to bring her disappointing news, especially given that she was lying in a hospital bed. But it seemed an equally bad time to lie to her.

"There were problems when we were in LA," I said. "I was going to quit, and Kelsey was going to shut down production, but I knew how important it was for Empirical."

"Oh, darling," said Mrs. Whitney. "You should never do something you don't want to do because someone else wants you to do it."

"We all wanted the show to go well," I said, "and it would have, except for Stella."

"I'm sure it's challenging for her, trying to fill your shoes, given that she's so intimidated by you," said Mrs. Whitney.

Stella Power, intimidated by *me*? That certainly had never been the way I'd seen it.

"Why would Stella be intimidated by me?" I said.

"You've got everything she wants," said Mrs. Whitney, in that decisive way that tolerated no contradiction. "You're independent, you're creative, and you've attracted the eye of that young man who plays opposite her in the show."

It took me a moment to realize that by "young man" she meant Hugo.

"I'm not sure you're right about that," I said. "But tell me about you. Are you going crazy in here?"

"I'm trying to see it as a chance to catch up on all the pleasure reading I never have time to do."

"What are you reading?"

"The rest of Proust," she said. "*Lincoln in the Bardo:* I'm a few years behind on that one. I hear great things about this young fantasy writer N. K. Jemisin."

"I could bring you some books," I said. "Or a Kindle. Have you tried reading on one of those?"

"Great for traveling," she said. "But you know, I'm a publisher. I love the paper, the fonts, the deckled edges, the *smell.*"

"I know," I said. "I feel like I never get to read anymore. Not an actual book, anyway."

"Books are wonderful," Mrs. Whitney said, "but it's life that's really important. Tell me about your world. How is life after *Younger*? Are you minding terribly not being a girl anymore?"

"That part's fine," I said, surprised I actually meant it. "It's a relief, actually. I like trying to figure out what this age is all about, because it's going to come and go too."

"Late forties, early fifties sounds so young to me," Mrs. Whitney said. "But it can be a dark time too."

"That's true," I said. "I didn't expect that."

"Oh yes," Mrs. Whitney said. "Your parents die, your children leave, you lose your job, no one looks at you anymore. It is the absolute nadir."

"Was it dark for you?" I asked, surprised to hear Mrs. Whitney confess to any weakness or low point. She always seemed so strong and in control.

"It was," she said. "My husband had died in a car crash at the same time the business was really taking off. Then I met someone. I guess you could say I fell in love. Her name was Helena Fletcher; she was an agent. The problem was she lived in London."

"She?" I said, surprised again.

"Yes. It seemed a terribly shameful secret at the time. Now I can't imagine why. So I pushed it away and put it off, and then the moment passed," she said.

I couldn't help thinking of Hugo. "Did you two stay in touch?"

"She died. Ovarian cancer. Not taking the chance to be with her is my one real regret. My life could have been so much richer."

"I'm so sorry," I said. "There was no one else?"

"I loved my husband, I loved her, and that was enough for me," she said. "I poured all my energy into my company."

"Having that passion, about someone or something, that's really enviable," I said.

"What about you, Liza?" she said. "Do you think you'll go back and work on the TV show, or write another book, or what?"

"I still feel like I'd like to work with other people, but not on the TV show," I said. "I'd love to find someplace I was as happy and comfortable as I felt working at Empirical."

"I wish I could make that time come back for your sake as well as mine," said Mrs. Whitney. "But all any of us have is now."

■ ■ ■ ■

It wasn't until I was on the train heading back to New Jersey that I remembered the envelope I'd delivered to Mrs. Whitney. I recalled her taking it from me. But I'd never found out what was inside.

I tried calling Mrs. Whitney's cell phone from the train, but she didn't pick up. I panicked a little but told myself she was probably off getting another of the endless tests she'd complained about. They kept you busy in the hospital.

I leaned back on the hard plastic seat and shut my eyes. The word *now* kept echoing in my brain. The time to do anything is now.

There was something undeniably comfortable for me, I realized, in not doing what I really wanted to do. As long as I was mired in doing something I *didn't* want to do, my dissatisfaction was justified and my dreams stayed safely on the shelf. Nothing was put to the test. I wasn't failing, I wasn't succeeding, I wasn't even really waiting, because waiting implied something else you were moving toward. I was living as a hologram of myself, my energy and passion in suspension until that day, that faraway day that never seemed to come, when I'd finally be doing what I really wanted. Never making myself find out what that was.

Denying the reality, year after year after year, that all I had was now.

In many ways, I realized, I still wanted to delay this reckoning. I should at least wait a couple of months, until the baby was a little older, and Caitlin and Ravi had their sea legs as parents. Or I could wait until she was a year old, ready for day care, maybe, by which point I might have managed to write a few sentences. Or until she was in kindergarten, or high school, or college.

I'd turned thirty, putting off my real adult life until some point in the future. I'd turned forty, waiting for the future. I could easily turn fifty doing the same thing. And fifty-five and sixty and seventy, waiting and waiting and waiting until it was too late. I wanted to keep waiting and never acting. Because it was less painful than trying my hardest and still not getting what I wanted.

After Eloise was bathed and settled in her bassinet, at least until eleven or twelve and her first nighttime feeding, Caitlin and Ravi curled up on the sofa with Netflix. This was my cue, I'd learned, to retreat upstairs to my third-floor room so they could have some couple time alone. I didn't resent that, in general. But it wasn't going to happen tonight.

"I need to talk to you," I said.

"I have some reading to catch up on," said Ravi.

"Both of you," I said.

I turned on the living room light and sat across from them.

"I love Eloise more than anything," I said, "and I really appreciate you trusting me with her welfare. I know you both are under a lot of pressure with your job and your fellowship. But I can't take care of her anymore."

They both frowned, which made me want to rush in and tell them I'd keep doing it till they found someone else, to offer to find someone for them, to stay while she learned the ropes.

I looked at the ceiling. Remembered the sky full of wonderful things. I'll take some courage, I thought. And some strength.

Caitlin burst into tears. "I knew you wouldn't really help me," she said. "You thought all along that I should stay home. You told me not to go for this job. And you know what, you were right, it is too hard. You say you can't do it, well, I can't do it either. I'm going to quit."

"You can't quit," Ravi said, horrified.

307

"We're depending on your income right now."

"You're going to have to give up that precious fellowship and get a job," she said, angry at him now.

"Neither of you have to quit," I said. "You can hire someone. There are lots of wonderful caregivers out there."

"I don't want a stranger in my house alone with my baby," Ravi said.

"Then a day care center that takes infants," I suggested.

I had actually googled all this on my phone on the train back from the city, to reassure myself that I wasn't leaving them without options.

"I'm not going to leave my newborn infant at some institution," said Caitlin.

"Well then, I'm not sure what to tell you," I said. "Ravi, you once talked about bringing the baby with you to school. Is that still a possibility?"

"I'm not sure," he mumbled.

"I can help you look for other options tomorrow, but first thing Monday I'm heading into the city."

I was going to help to successfully finish shooting the show. I hadn't told Kelsey this yet. The idea was still formulating, and I didn't want to get her hopes up in case I changed my mind or chickened out. If I showed up on set and she didn't want me there, then I'd figure out something else. Something that didn't involve reliving a former life.

"I wish you'd thought of this before you volunteered to come out here," Caitlin said.

I could have pointed out that I didn't exactly volunteer, but that would have been arguing the wrong point.

I took Caitlin's hand, and then reached for Ravi's too. Half to my surprise, he let me take it, and even gripped mine back a little.

"I saw the two of you, under the most difficult conditions any parent could face, being so strong and kind and brave and loving," I said. "You were the best possible parents to Eloise, straight out of the gate, and I have complete confidence that you are going to be amazing parents to her from now on, both of you."

"I've never even spent a single hour with her," Caitlin said.

"Are you kidding?" I said. "You barely left her side at the hospital."

"But there was always a nurse or a doctor there, or Ravi was there, or you were there. Someone was there to help me if I screwed up."

"I'll help you," Ravi said.

"You're not going to screw up if you take care of Eloise on your own, either of you," I said. "And you don't have to do it alone. You have each other, and there are all kinds of wonderful people you can hire, people who will enrich your child's life and who will make you feel confident about working. I'm proud of you both for having such successful careers, and that's not something selfish, that's something you're giving your daughter too."

Ravi squeezed my hand.

"Thank you, Liza," he said. "I appreciate all the time you spent with us, and all the help you gave us. It really meant a lot."

I was glad I was holding both their hands, because I might have fallen over.

"Well, thank you, Ravi," I said. "That's really nice of you to say."

"I appreciate it too," Caitlin said.

"I know you do, sweetheart."

"You know, some of the women I work with have read your book, and they thought it was so cool you were making it into a TV show with that Hugo guy, who is apparently some kind of big deal," Caitlin said. "They couldn't believe it when I told them you were taking care of the baby instead of doing that."

"Yeah, you should be working on the show and writing," said Ravi. "I get it. I know how important my career is to me. I love Eloise more than anything, but I don't want to step back from my career to be with her full-time."

"Oh really?" said Caitlin, withdrawing her hands. "So does that mean I need to be the one to step back?"

"Nobody needs to step back!" my son-in-law said. "Like your mother said, we can hire someone. . . ."

"But we're not going to be able to find somebody just like that," Caitlin said. "I can't take off from my new job after two weeks, to interview nannies."

Ravi had a rejoinder, but I didn't stick around to listen to it. I had packing to do. This was their problem, and it wouldn't be easy, but they would work it out. And work it out again and again over the years as their family and their positions changed. When you have a newborn, you think that's the hardest it's ever going to get, and then when you have a two-year-old or a teenager, you look back and you can't believe how easy it was before they walked, talked, or demanded an iPhone.

# TWENTY-FOUR

I got the cinematographer to send me the call sheet for Monday, then showed up at the waterfront street in Williamsburg where they were shooting. I got there about ten, when I figured they'd be finished with hair and makeup and ready to shoot their first scene. I stepped directly into this exchange between Kelsey and Stella:

**STELLA**
I quit!

**KELSEY**
You can't quit, you're fired.

**STELLA**
You can't fire me, I'm firing you!

**KELSEY**
I don't care, because I quit!

312

At that, Stella whirled around and stomped toward her trailer. Hugo ran after her. I don't think he even noticed I was there.

"What the . . . ?" I said to Kelsey.

Everyone else had moved as far as possible from us without abandoning the set altogether and seemed to be involved en masse in studying the equipment, the script, anything that would take their eyes off us.

"I mean it this time; I've had it," Kelsey said.

"What happened?"

"I've been telling you some of it, but not the worst," Kelsey said. "She arrives late, she leaves early, she won't wear what we have for her, she flubs her lines. And then today she refused to shoot the scene we had planned. Said she didn't feel like it."

"Jeez, that sounds terrible," I said. "Do you think she'll calm down and come back?"

"I don't care if she calms down," Kelsey said. "I meant what I said. I'm out."

"Come on, Kels. You're almost at the finish line. You can't give up now."

"Why not?" Kelsey said.

"For one thing, I just came back to work with you again. You can't leave me here alone."

"That's great news," Kelsey said. "Leaving you here alone is exactly what I'm going to do. If you can convince her to come back, you can shoot the last three scenes."

"I have no idea what I'm doing!" I said.

"You'll figure it out," Kelsey said, an uncomfortable echo of what I'd told poor Caitlin and Ravi. "I need to go stare at the ocean for several days."

And with that she left. And I was there alone. Now, it seemed, had finally arrived.

It was quiet inside Stella's trailer, which made me hesitate. What if she and Hugo were . . . ?

Oh, fuck it. I was sick of this. If they were, then I'd know once and for all what was actually happening. I knocked. The door opened and there stood Hugo, not Stella.

"Is Stella here?" I asked him.

"Hello," he said.

"Hi."

He was still blocking the doorway. The last time I'd seen him had been the day I left the show to take care of Eloise. He'd texted me after Kelsey informed him that I wasn't returning to the set. I'd confirmed that was true, and then I'd stopped responding. Thinking he might be having an affair with Stella was one thing; thinking they were having a baby together, quite another.

"What are you doing here?" he said.

"I'm, uh, taking over the show from Kelsey. I need to talk to Stella."

He studied me for a moment, then stepped back. I climbed into the trailer. It was so cold it was like stepping into the refrigerated room at Costco. Stella was reclining on a gray velvet chaise she must have had specially installed, with a fuzzy cream mohair blanket pulled up to her chin.

"You!" she cried upon spotting me. "It's all your fault!"

"*My* fault?" I said, astonished. "How can anything be my fault?"

"You did *something* to Hugo," Stella said, "which caused him to *forsake* me. . . ."

"I did not forsake you, Stella," Hugo said. He sounded like the patient but exhausted dad of a rebellious teenager.

"He forsook me," Stella insisted. "Forsaked? You're the genius writer, you tell me."

"I'm not following," I said.

"Barry was right," Stella said. "Barry said I didn't really want to work, and I don't."

"So why did you want to do this show?" I asked.

"Isn't it obvious?" she said. "For love."

"Oh," I said. "You mean so you and Hugo could be together."

Stella started laughing maniacally. "That's

315

hilarious," she said. "Hugo said that's what you'd thought. I guess my plan worked, then."

"Stella was using me as a cover," Hugo explained.

"A cover for what?" I truly couldn't imagine.

"For me and Tane, of course!" Stella said. She sat up on the chaise and tugged the blanket around her shoulders like a shawl. "I mean, it didn't start out that way. At first I *did* think I wanted to work, or at least I knew I wanted to get out of that fucking hellhole. . . ."

"By 'fucking hellhole,' " I said carefully, "do you mean your house in Malibu?"

"Duh," said Stella, rolling her eyes. She actually would have been good at playing a teenager. "So when Kelsey sent me your stupid book, no offense —"

"I thought you loved the book," I said, admittedly wounded.

"Love is what you say when you don't pass," Stella said. "Anyway, I thought it would (a) get me out of the hellhole, and (b) let everybody know I was still smoking hot."

"And then she thought maybe she could get even more out of the deal, isn't that right, darling?" said Hugo.

316

Even given the news that the two of them were not together, I felt a stab of jealousy hearing him call her "darling."

"First I thought I could make Barry jealous by insisting you hire Hugo, and when *that* didn't work —"

"It seems I have no credibility as the other man," Hugo explained to me.

"Barry knows Hugo's too much of a gentleman to fuck the boss's wife," Stella said.

"Absolutely true, by the way," said Hugo.

"As I now know," said Stella. "Instead of getting jealous, Barry decided that hinting at me and Hugo being back together would be a *fabulous* way to promote the show."

"Why didn't you just tell us that?"

"Barry didn't want to risk it getting around that it was all a fake," said Stella. "And then I had my own reasons."

"Which were?" I asked.

Stella sat there mutely, hugging the blanket. I couldn't take it anymore — I turned off the air-conditioning.

"You better tell her, or I will," said Hugo.

Stella rolled her eyes. "Then you ruined everything by making Hugo fall in love with you," she said. "So he refused to play the game anymore."

I could feel my cheeks flaming.

"You skipped a part," Hugo said to Stella, not looking at me.

I noted that he did not deny the "fall in love with" part.

"Okay, yes," Stella said. "Then I started fucking Tane, at first to *really* make Barry jealous, and then because, well, he's a god. I didn't want to go to New York because I didn't want to be so far away from him."

"And then you realized that if you came to New York, you could bring him with you," I said, dawn breaking.

"You got it," said Stella. "What surprised me was falling in love with *him*. I never thought I'd feel again the way I felt about you, dear Hugo."

"She's 'round the bend about the guy," said Hugo.

"I am 'round the bend and over the moon and crazy in love and I don't care who knows it," Stella said.

"Everybody's going to know it shortly," said Hugo.

"You mean because . . . that's right, I *am* having Tane's baby. And even if I were having sex with Barry, which I'm not, it would be clear the baby was not his, so why hide it? I've been married more than ten years, so according to California divorce laws, I get half. And if Barry tries to fight me on it,

318

I'll make *him* take the kids."

I couldn't tell if she was joking. Now that I was no longer worried about her and Hugo, I could refocus on what had brought me in here in the first place.

"What does all that have to do with finishing the pilot?" I said.

Stella seemed stumped for a moment, and then seemed to remember the reason. "There's no point in my finishing the pilot, is there?" she said. "Since I have no intention of doing the show."

"You're not going to do *Younger*?"

"That's right," she said.

"But what happens to our show?"

She shrugged. "Ask Barry. He owns the rights."

"You have to make him give them back to us," I said, furious.

Stella laughed. "I don't think he's going to care what I want right now."

"I'll go on shooting the rest of it, if that helps," Hugo volunteered.

"There's no show without me," Stella said.

I hated to admit it, but she was right.

She threw off the blanket and stood up, stretching and yawning.

"Ah, I feel so much better," she said, as if she'd just taken a peaceful nap.

I had to admit, as horrified as I was by

her behavior and what she'd done to our show, I was also impressed.

"This is the first time I've ever heard you say what you *really* think," I told her.

"I know, *right?*" she said. She gripped my arms and looked me hard in the eyes. "It's *amazing.* You should try it sometime."

# TWENTY-FIVE

I called Mrs. Whitney — I was very relieved to learn she was home from the hospital now — and broke the news to her that the show wasn't going to happen.

"I'm so sorry," I said. "I know you were counting on it as a way of bringing in some money."

"It doesn't matter now," she said, "because there's no more Empirical Press."

"What do you mean?"

"I don't have the energy to go on," she said. "I'm shutting down the publishing company."

"Wait a minute," I said. "What? No. You can't just close it down."

"I suppose I could sell the company — I've had lots of chances over the years — but I could never see one of those big conglomerates doing it justice," Mrs. Whitney said.

"I could help run the place until you're

feeling better. . . ."

"There's no money to pay you, Liza."

"You wouldn't have to pay me. Maybe we could work out some kind of partnership instead of a salary."

"You'd really want to do that?" Mrs. Whitney said.

"I would love to."

There was a long silence, then Mrs. Whitney said gently, "I'm not going back to work again, Liza. And without me, there is no Empirical."

It seemed unkind to keep arguing with her about what she did with Empirical Press. She'd created this firm from nothing and spent her whole life building it; it was her decision what became of it. In a day or two, when she was feeling stronger, maybe we could talk about it again.

"I just want to tell you, Mrs. Whitney," I said, a lump forming in my throat, "how much I admire you, and how much I've always looked up to you and tried to emulate you."

"Stop that," Mrs. Whitney said edgily. "That's something people do to you when you get older; they put you up on a pedestal. And I don't like it."

"I'm sorry," I said, stricken.

"Idealizing me like that is a way to keep

322

from getting close," Mrs. Whitney said. "It keeps you from seeing me as real."

She was right. I had done that. I was still doing it now. I wanted to see her as perfect, beyond wants and needs, because then I could believe that my life would also be like that one day.

"Can I come visit you?" I said. "I've never finished reading Proust either. I could read it out loud."

"Oh God, that sounds deadly," said Mrs. Whitney. "But you could come over and bring me a bottle of Taittinger's — rosé, please. You can tell me all about Hugo Fielding then, and I'll tell you about Helena."

She said she'd ask Betty to schedule a date.

When I saw Empirical Press on the ID of my phone the next day, I thought Betty was calling to arrange my champagne visit to Mrs. Whitney.

Instead Betty, actively weeping, told me that Mrs. Whitney had died. I calmly asked her details — when, what happened, where was the service — and carefully took down all the information. I thanked her, hung up, and then broke down, sobbing.

Mrs. Whitney didn't want her ghost to

linger, she'd said in her written instructions, so the memorial service was just a few days later, in the Trustees Room at the New York Public Library. Mrs. Whitney had planned the whole thing herself, when all those tests at the hospital had delivered the worst possible news: stage 4 pancreatic cancer, with a few months or maybe weeks to live. She'd only gotten days.

But even Mrs. Whitney made mistakes: She hadn't foreseen how many people would turn up at her own funeral, so they had to move the crowd twice, first to a larger meeting room, and then to Astor Hall, which held more than five hundred people.

Margaret Atwood spoke: Mrs. Whitney had published her early poetry. So did Jodi Picoult, Christina Baker Kline, and Benilde Little. The room was filled with writers and editors and publishers and *readers.*

I was standing with Kelsey and Maggie, listening to Sutton Foster — Mrs. Whitney's new friend, the person who *should* have played me — sing "I Will Survive." At first people tried not to laugh, but then we couldn't help it, the whole place broke down, dancing, singing, laughing, crying. Mrs. Whitney always had an excellent sense of irony.

I felt someone slip up beside me and take my hand: Hugo. He lifted my fingers to his lips and then held them there for so long he had stopped kissing and was just breathing. He gripped my hand in both of his through the whole service, as if he wanted to be sure I couldn't get away.

After the service was over, Betty appeared out of the crowd and gave me a big hug. Then she handed me an envelope. It was Empirical Press stationery, my full name written on it in Mrs. Whitney's handwriting. A shiver ran through me.

"Does this have something to do with the envelope I brought her in the hospital?" I said. "I never found out what was in that."

Betty shrugged, though she often knew more about everything than she let on.

"She gave it to me sealed and told me to get it to you, after . . ." Betty trailed off. "Well, here we are. Now you take care, dear. Let me know if you need anything."

The four of us — me, Kelsey, Maggie, Hugo — stood together on the steps outside the library.

"I could definitely use a drink," said Maggie.

"Bemelmans?" I asked.

When we'd settled into a corner booth, Kelsey said, "She brought me here when she told me she was making me editor."

"I was always jealous that you got to go out to lunch with her," I said.

"I was a senior editor," Kelsey said. "You were a little junior assistant."

"I was totally paranoid that Mrs. Whitney was going to recognize me from the first time I worked there. When I finally talked to her about it, after she knew the truth, she said we all looked alike, she never noticed anything!"

"I heard about Mrs. Whitney for years," Maggie said. "She was the woman Liza wanted to be when she grew up."

"I still do," I said, shaking my head. "What am I going to do without her as my role model?"

"You still have her," Hugo said. "You have her in here." He thumped his heart.

"What was in the envelope her assistant gave you?" Maggie asked.

I'd nearly forgotten about it.

"I'll read it at home," I said, figuring it was a personal letter from Mrs. Whitney, and I didn't want to start bawling, not yet.

"You can't hold out on us," said Kelsey. "Come on, it'll be like she's here with us."

I looked to Hugo for support. "Spill it," he said.

"I'll open it and start to read," I said, "and

if I'm comfortable sharing, I will, and if I'm not, I won't. Can everyone live with that?"

They grudgingly agreed.

I opened the letter and started reading.

"Holy shit," I said.

"Is it bad?" said Kelsey.

"The opposite of bad."

It was not a long letter, but nevertheless contained massive news.

*" 'My dear Liza,' "* I read.

*" 'Thank you for coming to see me today. Our talk made me realize something I never thought of before. Along with continuing to run Empirical Press or shutting it down, there was a third option: leaving it to you.' "*

When I read that line aloud, it felt real to me in a way it hadn't when I first read the sentence. I let out a yelp, or possibly more of a scream. Heads swiveled and everyone at our table started talking at once. But there was more in the letter, and I held up my hand to stop them. I needed to finish before we could really talk.

*" 'Think about whether you really want to take this on,' "* I read aloud. *" 'And if you do, I advise that you do it differently than I did and consider taking on a partner. I wish I had time to run the company in partnership with you as you suggested, but the next best thing is to imagine you doing it with someone else. Run-*

ning a business by yourself can get lonely. You need someone, at work and in life, who loves and supports your fullest self.'

" 'Of course, I'm also leaving you the cabin in Maine, but think about whether you really want that too. It's awfully far away and it's a tumbledown place, but it made me so happy that it proved so restorative for you. It's yours if you'd like, and perhaps in the future you'll pass it on to someone who appreciates it the way you do.'

" 'Also enclosed is the contract for the TV show. I was so embarrassed when I realized I'd forgotten to sign it, I wanted to explain in person at the hospital and sign it right away. When you told me how badly the show was going, I thought maybe I'd hold off. This is the only signed copy. You can send it in to the network or you can tear it up and nullify the deal. It doesn't matter to me anymore; do what's best for you.' "

"That little sneak!" Kelsey said. "She told me she'd sent it to Fernando, but then Fernando thought she'd sent it to Stella, and Stella said she had it, why were we bugging her. Meanwhile Mrs. Whitney was totally playing us!"

"Aren't you glad?" said Hugo.

As Kelsey and I watched openmouthed, he plucked the contract from my hand and

328

tore it up.

"I guess Whipple Studios doesn't own the TV rights to your book anymore," he said.

Kelsey and I looked at each other, then back at him.

"Without a valid contract," Kelsey explained, "all the rights revert to us. We can go out and remake the show with somebody else."

At exactly that moment, I thought I caught a glimpse of Sutton Foster walking through the hotel lobby.

I looked back at the letter, though I wasn't registering much anymore. But I made myself read the last paragraph.

" *'Give my love to that darling Hugo and clever Kelsey and your lovely daughter and granddaughter, and of course to yourself too. I am so sad that I have to say goodbye.'* "

I'd been sniffling throughout, but this is where I started full-on sobbing. My friends sat awkwardly for a moment, then Hugo moved closer and tried to put his arm around me. But he was in a chair, while I was at the end of the semicircular booth, so he couldn't really reach me, and the arm of the chair was getting between us. Finally, he got out of his seat and scooted in beside me, forcing everyone else to squish together when he put his arms around me. I smashed my face into his shoulder and let go.

# TWENTY-SIX

The fire in the big stone fireplace in the cabin in Maine was roaring. It was the week after Mrs. Whitney's funeral. I needed to get out of the city and take a big breath after everything that had happened. And I needed to have sex with Hugo. Mrs. Whitney's cabin seemed like the perfect place to do both.

We took turns driving the old Volvo up through New England. I didn't let anyone but Maggie know I was leaving town, but on the drive I texted Caitlin.

*How's everything?* I wrote.

*Good!* she wrote back. *Ravi's cooking his way through Sam Sifton and teaching himself Chinese.*

Ravi had taken his parental leave to stay home with Eloise while they looked for childcare. Ravi had always enjoyed doing what for other people would be impossible. Maybe he'd found his calling.

*I'm on my way to Maine to my new house,* I texted Caitlin.

My new house. The home I'd wished for the last time I left.

*Yay!* Caitlin texted back. Strangely, she seemed more relaxed and warmer to me since I'd left, so maybe this arrangement was better for her, too.

*Maggie's around if you need anything,* I wrote.

*You're alone?* Caitlin texted back.

I hesitated a moment before I answered, *With Hugo.*

Caitlin texted back the emoji of the hands clapping, the champagne cork popping, the woman dancing in the red dress, and then many hearts.

We left the Volvo in the usual parking lot and took the last ferry of the day over to the island, the early fall wind biting into our faces. It would start snowing soon; this was the last chance to be here until spring.

The first thing we did was build a big fire, which took about an hour to warm up the place. We ate some soup, still wearing our coats. When dark fell, we lit every candle we could find, which thankfully was not that many. I didn't really want it to be that bright in there. It was finally getting warm enough to contemplate taking off our clothes. But still I was shivering.

"We don't have to do this," Hugo said.

"Oh," I said. "I think we do."

We took a step closer to one another.

"We could get into bed and take our clothes off under the covers," I said.

"I want to see you," said Hugo.

"That's kind of my problem."

"What are you talking about?"

"What if you don't like the way I look?" I said.

"I will like the way you look."

I had put on some weight and lost a lot of muscle since I came down from this island six months before. Plus no matter how thin or strong I was, I was still nearly fifty. Getting older made me more secure in a lot of ways, I'd discovered, but not about my body.

"I have a stomach," I said. "My tits are saggy. I have cellulite all over my thighs."

He laughed. "Me too," he said.

He pulled his sweater over his head and started unbuttoning his shirt, moving his shoulders and his hips in some mimicry of a striptease, though he looked more like Elaine dancing on *Seinfeld*.

When his shirt was off, he held his arms out. "What do you think?" he said.

The only place I had ever seen a man over fifty with his shirt off was at the beach. And

Hugo looked . . . like those guys. His shoulders were a little hunched, the skin on his upper arms loose, his stomach paunchy. His chest hair was completely gray. He'd gotten a running start on his goal of eating whatever he wanted and not worrying about his weight. I reached out and laid my hands on his chest.

"You look beautiful," I said, and meant it.

He leaned down and kissed me, softly but insistently. The room suddenly grew a lot warmer.

"Okay, now for the big reveal," he said.

He had to sit down on the edge of the bed to take off his socks and shoes. Then, without ceremony, he unzipped his jeans and tugged them off. He was wearing black boxer briefs.

"Nice underwear," I said.

"I bought it specially," he told me.

He pulled the briefs down. His penis jumped out.

"Wow," I said. It was definitely impressive.

He kicked off the underwear and I moved over next to him. I ran my hands over his ass, then around to the front, trailing my fingers up to the tip of his penis and back down.

"If you keep doing that, this is going to be

over really quickly," he said.

I did not want it to be over quickly. We had waited so long. Which had created a lot of pressure. It was like we were the heroine and hero of a movie, and the whole story had been yearning toward this moment when we were finally together. And it had to be great. Well, in the movie, you didn't see them worrying about whether it was going to be great, or it not being great — it was always great. They were both so beautiful and they loved each other so much, plus they were movie stars: How could it not be great?

But in life, sometimes you could be with someone very attractive and who you really liked, and at the moment of truth, you might discover that you simply were not compatible in bed.

"You need to either take off your clothes now," said Hugo, "or you need to get into bed with them on, because any minute now I am going to have snow balls."

"The last night I was here, I slept with my clothes on," I said, leading him over to the bed. "Even my coat."

I remembered how cold it was that night, letting the fire die out for the last time before I rejoined civilization. Excited about everything that lay ahead, but never guess-

ing that six months later, I'd be back here
with Hugo Fielding.

"Come on," he said.

We crawled in together under the huge
feather comforter, which was topped with a
heavy wool blanket and on top of that, a
patchwork quilt. You could barely turn over
under the weight of those covers. It was like
sleeping under a bear.

Plus it was a double bed. And Hugo was a
big guy. We lay there for a minute, pressed
together, our arms wrapped around each
other. I could feel his heart beating against
mine. It took us both a moment to stop
quaking from the cold in the room. Although given that I still had all my clothes
on, my shivering may have been for another
reason.

"Are you a virgin?" Hugo said.

I laughed. "Born again."

"We could get married first," he said.

I froze. "What?"

"I want to marry you, Liza. Please marry
me. I'd get down on one knee, but then I'd
have to let go of you."

"Don't let go of me," I said.

"Is that a yes?"

"Let me think about it," I said. I kissed
him. And then I kissed him some more.
"Mmmm, yeah, this is helping me think."

Soon I was so hot I had to throw off the covers. I struggled to pull my sweater and turtleneck over my head and wiggle out of my pants. I'm not sure how my underwear came off. Once we were kissing, we moved nearly seamlessly (except for the turtleneck) to fucking. And once we were fucking, I was lost in the deliciousness of the physical feeling of that, like eating again at the end of a long diet, like the first warm day of spring, like the embrace that makes you realize how much you've missed being touched.

But what I felt with Hugo was like the first warm day of spring after a winter that had lasted three years. A day that was not only warm and sunny, but as vivid and brilliant and beautiful as the best days you've ever known. *How have I lived without this so long?* I wondered. *How can I ever bear to stop?*

We didn't stop, not for longer than it took to throw more wood on the fire and cook up a panful of bacon and take a brisk walk down to the water and back, if only to experience the pleasure of getting warm all over again.

At the end of the week, I checked if he'd been serious about the proposal. He said of course, and I said yes.

I felt something with Hugo that I'd never felt with Josh or with my ex-husband, either, though I didn't realize it until I was experiencing it. I felt like I was fully inside my body, and no part of me was standing outside judging, directing, criticizing, craving, feeling something different from what I was feeling. Wanting something different from what I had. Being someone different from who I was. There was no shadow me. There was just me. With him.

# TWENTY-SEVEN

Maggie and I invited everyone we'd ever known to our one hundredth birthday party in December, which we held at my new home, the smallest carriage house in Clinton Hill. It was so small, I couldn't believe they'd actually fit carriages and horses into it. Dogs, maybe? And I was renting it; I hadn't bought it. But it had a wood-burning fireplace and a spiral staircase that led to a tiny sleeping loft. Mine was the only name on the lease. I owned the cabin in Maine. And I finally had not one but two homes I'd always dreamed of.

Almost everyone showed up, from Maggie's *Nona,* who really was one hundred, to my granddaughter, Eloise, nearly six months old and so gorgeously chubby you would never have known she'd been a preemie.

I kissed her delicious little leg, which was dangling from the carrier her dad wore against his chest. She kicked and chortled.

Her hair, growing in now, was thick and dark, but in the right light I could pick up an unmistakable glint of red.

"How's my little munchkin?" I said.

Eloise threw her head back, consumed by laughter.

"Happy birthday, Mom," my daughter said, giving me a hug.

"Hey, sweetie. Did you get some champagne?"

"Not for me," Caitlin said.

She and Ravi traded glances.

"We have some news," Caitlin said, a smile playing at her lips.

"What?"

Eloise was still so tiny, it took me another moment to catch on.

"What?!?" I said again, astonished. "When?"

"August," Caitlin said. "Fingers crossed I make it that far."

"I calculated that if we had another baby right away, we could minimize the time I'll need to defer my fellowship and maximize the financial advantage of me being primary caregiver," Ravi explained.

I felt a twinge of guilt about Ravi's deferring his fellowship, but reminded myself that stepping back from his career to care for the baby had been his choice, as it had been mine with Caitlin and not with Eloise. And believing in choice meant you supported it whether someone's choice conformed to your personal beliefs or not.

"Ravi thinks if we invest everything we would have spent on childcare, we can build up a healthy college fund," Caitlin said.

"Very smart," I said. "I'm so thrilled. See you Wednesday?"

Wednesday was my day with Eloise, starting early in the morning and stretching into the evening, when Caitlin and Ravi went out on their date night. Spending that one long day a week with the baby both made me wish I could spend more time with her, and underscored my decision not to.

"Thank you," said Ravi, who'd been humbled by his tenure as a stay-at-home dad, not necessarily a negative. "We really appreciate it."

Caitlin and Ravi turned toward another admirer of Eloise's then, in time for me to see Kelsey slip into the room. She was, I was surprised to note, alone.

"Where's Josh?" I asked her.

She shrugged. "I'm not sure."

"I thought you two were coming together," I said.

She shrugged again. That was when I noticed tears glistening in her eyes. "It looks like we might have broken up," she said.

"Oh no!" I'd thought Josh and Kelsey were perfect together. "What happened?"

"We love each other," she said. "But we're not sure we *love* each other, if you know what I mean."

I wasn't sure I did, but I told her I was sorry to hear that. "I thought you two would get married and make beautiful babies."

"I don't know about the marriage part, but the babies might still be on."

"What? Really?"

She smiled, nodding. "I haven't said anything to him because things have been so weird, but I took a test." She nodded again. "What do you think of the name Hope?"

"Oh, Kelsey!" I gathered her into a hug.

"What are you ladies whispering about now?" It was Stella, but I swear I almost didn't recognize her. Six months pregnant now, she had gained at least a hundred pounds, but also looked a hundred times happier. She gave both Kelsey and me big kisses on the lips.

Tane stood shyly back, looking ill at ease in his winter clothes. The knit of his sweater parted at the shoulders, and his massive thighs threatened to pop the seams of his chinos. Not that I noticed or anything. He and Stella were living full-time at the Dakota now and were said to be shopping for a place in Montauk. She had, after all, gotten the kids, who were settled in New York City public schools.

"Guess what!" Stella grabbed me by the shoulders and shook me until my teeth rattled. "I'm writing a book!"

"Congratulations," I said cautiously. Stella's memoir had incited a bidding war among publishers, one that Empirical had sat out. Stella had pulled down a seven-figure advance, way more money than I hoped to ever earn from writing, even if I lived to be two hundred.

"Writing is hard!" she said. "I would really love your help."

"My help?" I said. "What kind of help do you need from me?"

"I know exactly what I want to say," she said. "I just need some help with getting the words down."

"I'm sure your agent and publisher can help you find a ghostwriter," I said coolly.

"But I want *you*," she said, making a little pout.

"I wish I could," I said. "I just don't have the time."

And I never will.

"Really?" she said, as if that were a totally

absurd idea. "What are you up to these days?"

"I'm running the publishing company now, and . . ." Smiling shyly, I held out my ring finger.

"Wow," she said. "Is that real?"

"Yes, Hugo and I are engaged."

She actually looked impressed.

"Hello, darling." Speak of the devil. Hugo kissed me on the cheek and held out a glass of champagne. His bump was nearly as big as Stella's. He'd been spending a lot of time cooking since he officially moved into my carriage house. He and Maggie worked side by side on the Sunday dinners now, and it turned out his extra girth not only made him even more attractive to me, but had actually proved to be an advantage in the theater. He was opening in his first play on Broadway next month.

"Do you have one of those for me?" Stella said, gesturing toward the champagne.

"I didn't think you were drinking," Hugo said.

"It would be bad luck if I didn't take a sip for the birthday toast," Stella said smoothly.

Hugo shrugged and glided away.

"I hear you're making *Younger* without me after all," Stella said.

Mrs. Whitney's failure to sign and return

344

the contract indeed gave us back the rights. We made a deal with dream producer Darren Star, who was here tonight with dream star Sutton Foster. After officially denying *Younger* was a memoir for so many months, I was now tripping over myself to let people know *Younger* was based on a true story, and that the main character was me. I even gave her my real name.

Maggie stepped forward, motioning for me to join her. She slipped her arm around my waist.

"Thank you all for coming to help celebrate Liza's and my first hundred years," she said.

A hundred years. That went so fast.

Would I change anything? Looking around the room at all the people I loved and who loved me, it was impossible to imagine wanting even a single moment to be different. Everything had to happen exactly the way it did to bring me to this wonderful place.

So all things considered, my first half century had gone perfectly. Given all I'd learned in my first fifty years, the next fifty promised to be even better.

# ACKNOWLEDGMENTS

I was supported through every stage of creating this book by two amazing allies: my agent, Johanna Castillo of Writers House, and my editor, Kate Dresser at Gallery Books. They both contributed the kind of insight, strength, strategy, good sense, and all-around brilliance that writers dream about.

I also owe tremendous gratitude to Darren Star, the genius who swooped from the sky and transformed my novel *Younger* into a new work of art. Darren, along with the fantastic writers and actors of *Younger* and TV Land's Keith Cox, have in every sense made my dreams come true.

To the magical Sutton Foster, the brilliant Hilary Duff, the soulful Debi Mazar, and the dreamboat Nico Tortorella, who brought the major characters from my original book to life so vividly and beautifully: your performances couldn't help but inspire my vision for the future of Liza, Kelsey, Maggie, and Josh. And to Peter Hermann and Miriam Shor, whose characters were Darren's brainchildren, I found a way to give you some much-deserved applause, too.

Producers and writers Dottie and Eric Zicklin, Alison Brown, and Ashley Skidmore have built the world of *Younger* out far beyond the imagination of any one writer, so with *Older* I had to dive far ahead in time to find a fresh story.

At Gallery Books, along with the brilliant and insightful and kind editor Kate Dresser, I'd like to thank editorial director Aimée Bell, my fairy godmother, as well as Molly Gregory and Lauren Truskowski.

*Younger* has had a long life, and I have to thank the agents and editors who had a hand in nurturing it along the way: editors Amy Pierpont and Lauren McKenna, agents Deborah Schneider and Melissa Flashman, as well as, on the TV side, Dana Spector at CAA.

Writing a novel is a long process that starts months or even years before you write the first word. Special thanks to my son, Owen Satran, who first broke down the elements that evolved into this book; Christina Baker Kline, who told me that whatever I wrote had to be funny and introduced me to my wonderful agent, Johanna Castillo; and to my LA BFF, Kate Juergens, who listened to me rant, postulate, complain, crow, worry, and wonder throughout the writing of this book, and responded with calm, clarity, creativity, and wisdom.

Thanks to Jesse Calhoun, who summoned the magic along with the bird. (I live in Los Angeles, where these things are real.)

Other friends, supporters, and colleagues who helped give Liza a new life include: Alex Enders and Verlyn Klinkenborg, Alexa and Claude Garbarino, Amy Neiman, Charlene and Tom Hajny, Danielle Roderick and Josh Parkinson, Deborah Gilbert, Denise Rue, Elizabeth Condon, Henry Seltzer, Jeannie Ralston, Justine Goodman, Kendall Wilkinson, Kim Bonnell and Michael Sukin, Laurie and Frank Albanese, Sarah Haberman, and Wendy Smith.

To my family, Rory and Joe Satran, Nathaniel and Plum Kilcer, love forever.

# ABOUT THE AUTHOR

**Pamela Redmond** is the *New York Times* bestselling author of more than twenty works of fiction and nonfiction, including *Younger, How Not to Act Old,* and *30 Things Every Woman Should Have & Should Know.* She started publishing novels, cofounded the world's largest baby name website *Nameberry,* got divorced, moved from New Jersey to Los Angeles, and changed her name, all after the age of fifty. The mother of three and grandmother of one, Redmond's website is at PamelaRedmond.com.